INVITATION
TO THE GAME

INVITATION TO THE GAME

Monica Hughes

SIMON & SCHUSTER BOOKS FOR YOUNG READERS
Published by Simon & Schuster
New York • London • Toronto • Sydney • Tokyo • Singapore

SIMON & SCHUSTER BOOKS FOR YOUNG READERS
Simon & Schuster Building, Rockefeller Center
1230 Avenue of the Americas, New York, New York 10020
Copyright © 1990 by Monica Hughes
All rights reserved including the right of reproduction in whole or in part in any form. Published by arrangement with HarperCollins*Publishers Ltd.,* Toronto. SIMON & SCHUSTER BOOKS FOR YOUNG READERS is a trademark of Simon & Schuster. Designed by Vicki Kalajian. Manufactured in the United States of America.   10 9 8 7 6 5 4 3 2

Library of Congress Cataloging-in-Publication Data
Hughes, Monica. Invitation to the game / by Monica Hughes. p. cm. Summary: Unemployed after high school in the highly robotic society of 2154, Lisse and seven friends resign themselves to a boring existence in their "Designated Area" until the government invites them to play The Game. [1. Science fiction.] I. Title. PZ7.H87364In 1991 [Fic]—dc20 90-22832 CIP   ISBN 0-671-74236-1

CONTENTS

ONE

April 2154. The Last Rites

It was the last day of school and the terror of the previous weeks had crept up on me again. My classmates were already gathering in the Assembly Room for what we jokingly called the Last Rites, and I had run upstairs to the dormitory for my journal, forgotten under my pillow in the excitement of the Last Day.

I was only just in time. The domestic robots were already busy stripping the beds, bundling up the sheets for the laundry, and folding the blankets into neat rectangles, each topped by a pillow, to be placed on the mattresses. I rescued my journal from the robot's claw and stood with it tight against my chest, staring out of the window, trying to control my shivers.

The Government School, which had been my home for the last ten years, had been built three hundred years before in what would later become part of a national forest. From the dormitory window I could see softly rolling hills, the morning mist caught in their folds, and a small grove through which ran the road connecting the school with the main highway, out of sight somewhere beyond the trees and the mist.

A small procession of electric buses appeared from among the trees and scrunched up the gravel road to park in front of the main entrance. At the sight of them panic gripped me. My mouth was dry and my stomach churned. Within the next few hours I would be aboard one of those buses, heading off into the unknown, to some place where I would have to spend the rest of my life doing . . . doing what? I pressed my head against the cold glass and longed to be someone else, somewhere else, some*time* else. . . .

"Lisse, are you there? Lisse!"

I jumped and looked around, and the terror drew back, like a wild beast held temporarily at bay, because Benta was standing behind me, her smile wide, her eyes shining. Benta, my best friend for the last ten years.

"Oh, how you startled me. I was thinking. . . ."

"I'm sorry. You're white as a sheet. I missed you downstairs and guessed you'd be up here, dreaming as usual. Come on, or we'll be late for the Last Rites."

She caught my hand and pulled me out of the dormitory and along the echoing passage to the main stairs. The school was in an enormous house that had once been the estate of a nineteenth-century industrialist, back in the days when there were still such things as riches and servants; but it had long ago lost its elegance as generation after generation of children had trampled its corridors and crowded the classrooms and dormitories.

Only now, in the rare moment in which the hall was

empty, I caught a glimpse, as we ran down the wide, curving stairs, of what it might have been like two hundred years before. The carved stone arch. The delicate tracery of the fanlight above the great door. The pattern of tiles on the floor of the great hall. I tried to imagine a single family living here. One family, with human servants. No robots anywhere.

The Assembly Room was packed, the entire student body present to witness the awarding of diplomas to the hundredth graduating class in the school's history. Benta and I scurried up the aisle and took our places in the second row with our friends. There was Scylla's bright hair. Karen's quirky smile. Trent's frown. We'd spent ten years growing up together.

"In an hour it'll all be over," Benta whispered. "I'll be off home to the farm and you'll be set on an exciting career."

"*Me?* Oh, Benta, don't tease. The others, maybe. But me? I'll be lucky if—"

"Please stand for the Chairman of the Trustees," the robot-principal rasped. We rose obediently as the Chairman entered from the back of the stage. He was a big man, running to fat. I had no idea what he did for the rest of the year, but during the fourth week of March he appeared at the school for the Last Rites, and for the last nine years we had listened to him deliver the same speech. But this year his words had a new and immediate significance.

". . . you have completed an education that will fit you

splendidly for the challenges of the twenty-second century."

Will it? I wondered. I knew that this school used to have a ninety percent success rate in job placement, one of the best in the country. We were lucky to have been sent here, we were told. Now, rumor whispered, that rate had plummeted to a low of ten percent. *Ten* percent success! What chance would I have, with little more than dreams and a love of reading? I wasn't like Rich or Benta. Their futures were already secure. Rich would join his father's psychiatric practice and Benta would go to her father's farm. Even Alden and Katie were bound to be all right. Even though they had been taken from unemployed parents, like most of us, there must still be jobs available for first-class chemists and geologists.

The Chairman finally droned to his usual conclusion and we responded with a polite pit-pat of applause as he took his seat. Then an electrifying silence fell over the Assembly Room. My hands were damp and cold. *I mustn't faint,* I told myself desperately, and felt Benta's hand over mine, warm, comforting. The moment had come.

One by one, our names were called by the robot-principal. One by one, we climbed the flight of stairs to the stage, and received our diploma and an ominous white envelope from the claws of the principal.

It took almost an hour to process the one hundred and forty-eight students who were to graduate this year, the biggest class in the school's history. By the time the last name had been called, the white envelope containing my future status was limp in my damp hands.

At last the robot-principal retired to the side of the stage and the Chairman took the podium. He talked gracefully and briefly about a brighter future tomorrow and wished us luck in our new life. As he sat down, the younger students began to shuffle out. For them it was back to class, the excitement over for another year.

I pulled the printout from my envelope. The letters and numbers swam in front of my eyes. Panic overwhelmed me. I swallowed and blinked the text back into focus.

English	97%
Philosophy	85%
Biology	71%
History	70%

and so on down the list of subjects. I had done better than I had expected. Maybe it was going to be all right. Maybe there would be a job out there for me after all. I had left my options wide open, not overreaching myself with false hopes. Surely with these marks there should be something. Anxiously I scanned the sheet.

CAREER OPPORTUNITIES

Teacher: position robotized. Senior advisors only.

Nursing: oversupplied. Preventative medicine and public health care carried out by nurse robots.

And so it went down the list, past hairdresser and waitress, truck driver and janitor. Beside each occupation was the same comment: "Overcrowded. Work performed more cheaply and efficiently by robots."

Robots! The saviors of civilization, we'd been told often enough in history class. When pollution had almost destroyed the human race over a hundred and fifty years ago, they had taken over the task of keeping the industrial world running. But that was in the past. There were lots of kids growing up now. So why didn't they stop making the robots and give us a chance? It didn't make sense.

At the very bottom of the printout was a message:

CONGRATULATIONS ON GRADUATING WITH HONORS!
ENJOY YOUR LEISURE YEARS!
USE THEM CREATIVELY.

"Enjoy your leisure years." That was the fatal phrase. School was over and I was discarded, thrown out with the trash before I'd had a chance. But the others? As I looked up, my eyes suddenly swimming, the robot-principal trundled back to center stage and gave its customary attention-getting pseudo cough.

"For those of you who have failed to obtain work, welcome to the ranks of the unemployed. There is no cause for alarm. Your basic needs will be provided through the generosity of your Government. You will be bused to the area assigned as your future living zone, and you will be provided with credits sufficient for meals and shelter.

In addition you *are* free to eat in any Government cafeteria."

At a groan from a class clown, a weak ripple of laughter ran through the class. The robot, of course, went on talking in precisely the same tone of voice.

"It's really going to be a pleasure to get away from that humorless *drone*," Alden muttered.

"You think you won't be surrounded by robots in your future life? Get real! Shoulder to shoulder in your Government lab . . ."

"If I thought that, Trent, I'd retire from chemistry right now. Well, I suppose I'd better see where I've been assigned. Hope it's a good facility."

As he ripped open his envelope, the robot's voice broke in. "The buses will begin departing in twenty-eight minutes precisely. Each bus is numbered. You will find the corresponding number in the upper left-hand corner of your envelope. Please be ready to board your designated bus immediately."

My envelope had dropped to the floor. I picked it up. *Number three.*

"I'm on three too." Benta was bubbling with excitement. "At least we'll have some more time together to . . . oh, Lisse, you didn't get a job, did you? I'm so terribly sorry."

I tried to smile. "'Welcome to the ranks of the unemployed' it says here. Oh, well, I *was* expecting it. In a way." I tried not to let the bitterness seep into my voice. Benta was my best friend, but at this moment I almost hated her. *It isn't fair.* Why should she be secure, going home to her family farm in the Midwest, while I ...

"I wish you could come with me. I'll miss you, Lisse."

I managed a smile. "If I ever get hold of a travel voucher I'll come and see you."

"Oh, yes. We'll fatten you up. Fresh cream and eggs and lamb. Maybe Dad could get permission for you to stay and work."

I did laugh at that. "I'm not sure I could stomach cleaning out the barn or whatever it is you have to do. But thanks for the thought."

We were moving with the crowd now, out into the hall, through the open front door, and onto the gravel driveway where the five buses sat recharging their batteries.

A long black Toyota-Cad crunched over the gravel and parked directly in front of the door. "Mine, I believe." Richard elbowed his way between Benta and me. "So sad, all these good-byes. *Dear* Lisse!"

"So you're off, Rich?"

"As you say. Home in a couple of hours, if we don't hit a riot."

"Then more school, I suppose? You don't become a psychiatrist overnight, do you?"

"Not quite. But I *have* been working intensively with sleep-learn tapes all the time I've been studying medicine at school. I'll be apprenticed to my father until I get my own license to practice."

"Let's hope you never run out of clients." I tried to keep the dislike out of my voice. My eyes searched the crowd for Scylla and Karen and the others. Drat Rich!

"Dear Lisse, psychiatry's a gold mine! I ask you . . . High unemployment. Boredom. Low self-esteem. I'll have clients beating a path to my door. Your loss is my gain. Good-bye, dear Lisse, dear Benta."

Benta shook his hand firmly. "Good-bye, Rich. I wish you all the luck you deserve."

"I second that, *dear* Rich."

He took our wishes at face value. "Thank you both. I look forward to a rewarding and busy future." The car door slammed. The Toyota-Cad eased through the crowd and we boarded our bus.

"The last day of school *is* sad," Benta remarked thoughtfully as we took our seats. "But at least we won't ever have to listen to Rich pontificating again."

"Unless we break down and are assigned to him. Oh, imagine it!"

"I'd sooner take tranks or be brain-changed by the thought police, wouldn't you?"

"A tranquilizer's certainly preferable to Rich. But brain-changed . . ." I shivered.

The door slammed. As the bus started, I turned for one last look at the building that had been our home for the last ten years, the only real home we'd had since Childcare had taken us from our parents for "education." Why had they bothered, I wondered drearily. It was almost noon and a watery sun caught the stone façade and turned it a warm gold.

"Hold tight," warned the driver as he swung the bus off the privately maintained road leading to the school and

onto the main highway. We lurched from pothole to pothole, crashing down on the springs until I thought the
suspension would go, leaving us stranded.

We hung on for dear life, hardly able to talk for the
noise. I tried to look behind me and see if any others of
our friends were on the same bus. I'd missed them, talking to Rich. Would I ever see them again? Benta was
talking and I leaned close to hear her above the rattle of
the bus.

"Lisse, we haven't passed a single vehicle. I thought
this was a main road."

"Maybe it's true what they said — that there really is no
travel at all without special permission. Oh, Benta, once
you're home you won't be able to leave either. Stuck there
for the rest of your life."

"I won't mind, honestly. It will be home. But you . . ."

"I just can't imagine . . ."

"What?" she shouted in my ear as the bus bounced
over the potholes.

I shook my head and bit my lip. Staring through the
window at the low hills lurching by, I wondered where
the bus would stop for me, where I was supposed to go,
what I was supposed to do. *DA . . . designated area.* That
was where I was going. Would I be alone? Or would some
of my friends be there too? I doubted it. They were all so
sharp, there'd be jobs for them.

The trees thinned. The hills flattened. The greenery
slowly became gray. There were houses. And more
houses. Packed in rows like cartons on a shelf. We
stopped at some kind of checkpoint and the driver

wound down his window and handed over a manifest. It was read, handed back, and the bus was waved on.

I had a momentary glimpse of a young upturned face, a man no more than a couple of years older than me, his eyes cold and bored beneath a gray peaked cap. Then we were off again, moving down a city street that was in much better condition than the highway.

The next time the bus stopped was on a street lined with factories and warehouses. A gray street. Gray buildings. A gray and drizzling sky. Not a tree or a blade of grass. Something darted out of the shadows of an alley. I couldn't tell whether it was a very skinny cat or a large and well-fed rat.

The driver stood up and began to call names. Nobody I knew well. Ten kids moved to the front of the bus. The driver handed each of them a card. Wordlessly he opened the door to let them off, slammed it almost on the heels of the last, and started up again. I had a glimpse of them standing huddled together on the gray pavement. Their faces looked as hopeless as if they had been condemned to death.

We drove along shabby gray streets for about half an hour before the bus stopped again. The names he called were those of my friends. Scylla. Karen. Trent. Alden. Katie. Paul. And Brad. I realized with a sinking feeling in my stomach that I'd never see Brad again.

"Lisse, didn't you hear? He called your name too. Good-bye. Good luck."

"Good-bye, Benta. Oh, how I'll miss you."

We hugged each other. The tears in Benta's eyes

couldn't cancel out the happiness that glowed in her face. I tried to swallow my envy as I followed the others up the aisle.

The driver had swung the door open. Now he suddenly peered through the windshield and slammed it shut again. He swore under his breath.

A group of youths had erupted out of a side street directly in front of the bus. They were dressed in garish colors and their faces were masked, or perhaps painted— it was hard to tell through the dingy glass.

"Look out, driver. They've got weapons," Trent called over his shoulder. He'd been standing on the step, ready to leave.

"Just sticks, I think. Or metal bars." Brad's matter-of-fact voice was supposed to be comforting. *Metal bars*! What if they attacked the bus? But they ignored us and made for the windows of a store on our left. There was the sound of breaking glass and a scream. Now they were back, a woman struggling in their grip.

"Do something, damnit!" Brad yelled at the driver. "Open the doors and let us out to help."

"No *way*, kid. Forget it."

An enormous shadow came between us and the pale, watery sky. A deafening noise, the clatter of blades, and a helicopter dropped out of the air to settle directly in front of the bus. Armed men in gas masks spilled from it. We could hear the dull pop of exploding canisters. One by one the members of the gang collapsed and were dragged aboard the helicopter. Within two minutes the street was deserted and the copter was soaring above the rooftops.

"Ugh, smell that!"

"Stun smoke, I bet."

"Thought police. That was quick. How did they *know?*"

As everyone exclaimed, I remembered my readout . . . "Enjoy your leisure years. Use them creatively." . . . Three hours and a lifetime ago. I was sixteen years old and I might live to be sixty, if a gang didn't get me first. Forty years in this jungle? I felt unbearably helpless.

Was that why those kids painted their faces and rampaged through the city, breaking windows and carrying off women? Because violence was better than forty years of nothing? Even at the risk of being caught by the thought police?

The acrid smell had almost vanished. The driver slapped the door open. "Get going, you people."

I took the plastic card he thrust into my hand and followed the others down the steps. Behind me the door slammed. I had a quick glimpse of Benta's white face, the freckles standing out startlingly. Then the bus was gone, broken glass scrunching under its tires. I took a foolish step after it, waving.

"Lisse, where's our Lisse?" Scylla swooped down on me and swept me into the circle of her arms. "Don't wander off like that, child. This is the dark wood, full of wolves. We've got to stick together."

"We?" From the comfort of Scylla's arms I looked at the faces of the others. Each had a plastic card.

"Aren't you going to jobs? You're not *all* unemployed? I thought—"

"That you were the only one?" Alden laughed shortly, without humor.

"But, Alden, *you*? With your marks in chemistry and the work you were doing in plastics—"

"I know. I didn't even bother to look at my marks at first, can you believe it? But it seems the Government's not interested in new ideas."

"That's the problem with this society," Trent exclaimed. "It *is* uninterested. Dead in the water. We should scrap it and start over."

"How?" Karen asked, her big voice booming. "Societies tend to go on until they run down by themselves or rot from inside."

"Can you afford to wait that long?" Trent pushed his sharp face aggressively at Karen. "*I* can't."

"Don't talk like that, Trent. Suppose *they* hear." I looked over my shoulder. Scraps of trash blew down the streets. It *looked* empty. But how could you tell? I'd heard that the thought police were everywhere.

Scylla broke into her wonderful warm laugh. "So serious! On our first day of freedom! It's these dreary uniforms. Come on. Let's find this rehabilitation center we're supposed to report to." She held up her plastic card. "We'll get new clothes and a place to stay and a hot meal. Then we'll plan a strategy for living, and the world will suddenly be a less frightening place. You'll see."

"We? You mean *all* of us?" Scylla was right. The world *was* a less frightening place already.

Brad looked up from his card. "It's just over there."

We found ourselves standing in front of a door solid enough to withstand a siege. The high windows were heavily barred. The door opened only after we had all given our names and numbers.

Inside was artificial light and a grudging warmth. The smell of institution stew battled with institution disinfectant. But behind the desk there was a human being to greet us. If you could call it a greeting.

"Another bunch of you? It's going to be difficult to find somewhere for all of you to live. Eight? Oh, I don't know." She made a show of stabbing a few letters on her keyboard and shrugged.

"Somewhere we can all be together," said Scylla thoughtfully. "It's the sensible thing to do." She turned to the rest of us. "The only way we're going to survive in this jungle is by sticking together—that's obvious. Fate brought us together. Now we must take over from fate and make it permanent."

"You mean you'll share your credits? Oh, that's a different story."

"An old factory, perhaps, or a warehouse. With decent light for my painting."

"Close to a library."

"We could partition it up."

Excitedly, we began to see the possibilities.

The computer, quite unmoved by our enthusiasm, rejected the possibility of people living, rather than producing goods, in a factory. We had to invent a corporation and claim we all worked for Scylla, who would be designing paintings and wallhangings for the working rich. Apparently, the unemployed could do things like that. Almost instantly the terminal spewed out a printout with five addresses.

"All within your designated area. See, here's the map. You'd better each have a copy. Ignorance of the law is no excuse. If the police catch you outside your DA without a proper permit you've had it."

"So that's what *designated area* really means," Trent spat out. "Another word for prison."

"I don't understand why we can't live where we want, look for work ourselves, if it comes to that," Paul added. If there's trouble, I thought, it'll come from those two. Bad enough apart, together they're like one of Alden's explosive brews.

"Live where you *want*?" The receptionist was scandalized. "That'd be anarchy, wouldn't it? We can't have thousands of you unemployeds running around wherever you like, up to goodness knows what kind of mischief. And if you want a meal you'd better hurry up. The dining room closes in another five minutes. We'll give you dormitory space for three nights. After that you're on your own. No excuses. All right?"

The cafeteria food was so much like school meals that I wondered if there were a huge robot kitchen somewhere, dishing out stew for every institution in the country; but it was hot and it helped displace the lump of ice in the pit of my stomach.

Ignoring the drab surroundings and the gray stew,

Scylla spread her DA map out on the table and began to mark off the addresses we had been given. Two were at the boundaries of our DA and Brad dismissed them instantly. "It'll be like a war zone there, raiding gangs and so on . . . not exactly peaceful."

"How do you know?"

"Stands to reason. Each group has a DA. That automatically makes us territorial. After a time that gets to be important. If anyone steps over the line there's trouble. And there are always people who get their kicks out of trouble."

"Brad's right," Karen put in. "The Government is handling this problem very cleverly."

"What problem?"

"Us. The unemployed. Think about it. Our school alone dumped over a hundred people in the city in a single day. Think of all the Government schools around the country. There must be thousands and thousands of us."

"If we could just get together." Trent hit the table with his fist. "It'd be dynamite. We could overcome *anyone*."

"That's *why* we're in designated areas. We won't *ever* meet one another. We won't *ever* have the chance to get together and demand fairer treatment. They're really very clever," Karen added thoughtfully.

"I see. Divide and conquer. They just put a few new people at a time into a DA. They know we'll be too busy just surviving and learning the rules—"

"Rules, Brad? There don't seem to be any, except for sticking inside our DA."

"I don't mean Government rules, Paul. I mean *gang* rules."

That silenced us for a while. Then Scylla flicked her coppery hair back from her face. "Come on. There are three possibilities here. Two of them close to a public library and a Government food store. Let's go, chickens. And on the way we'd better find a Government clothing store—I feel terribly conspicuous in this uniform. Let's get out of these things and into something wonderful. If we can't be workers, at least we'll be decorative non-workers."

Infected by her enthusiasm, we surged out of the center onto the gray and gritty street, a kind of artificial high covering the fear that had crept up on us in the dingy cafeteria. Remembering the gang we'd seen from the bus and Brad's all-too-persuasive scenario of territorial wars, we walked along, the eight of us close together, looking over our shoulders and approaching corners with care. But there was no one around except a couple of workers in blue overalls who looked at us suspiciously and hurried by, more afraid of us, I thought, than we might be of them.

We found the clothing store only three blocks away. Once inside we kicked off our black sandals and got out of our gray pants and tunics. We wandered around, pulling clothes off the shelves, trying them on and discarding them until we drove the robot servers crazy. At last Scylla took us in hand, choosing our colors. Within an hour, we were all as resplendently clothed as the peacocks they say used to live here long ago.

Only Brad insisted on a sober jacket and pants of dark blue with a turtle neck to match. "I'd feel silly in all that fancy stuff," he said gruffly.

I thought he looked wonderful, but Scylla laughed. "They'll take you for a worker, if you're not careful," she teased. "You'll start getting privileges like train tickets and passes to real restaurants."

We walked out of the store, leaving our discarded uniforms to be picked up by the robot clerks, our past lives to be shredded and recycled. We took nothing with us except our new plastic ID cards and me my journal, which I tucked into the pocket of my cherry red . . . I almost said "uniform." I suppose it was a uniform, in a way. The un-uniform uniform of the unemployed.

"Don't you feel conspicuous, Scylla? I do," I said as we walked through the streets to the place where the first factory was situated. We passed a few shabby-looking shops, and an occasional shadowy figure peered at us through the grillework that protected the doors. "I've got the feeling we've no right to be here, and these clothes aren't much camouflage, are they?"

"If all the unemployed wear clothes like ours," Katie put in, "we must all show up like crows in a field of snow."

"Perhaps that's why the Government gave us the choice of such gorgeous colors."

"I bet you're right, Lisse. The thought police could spot us a mile away in these togs. Typical," Trent added.

Brad suddenly stopped and, since he had been leading the way, we all piled into him.

"What's up? Did you see someone?"

"No, I didn't. But, if we're so visible, how come we haven't seen another unemployed? Where are they all?"

As soon as Brad said it, it was obvious. It was almost as if we'd been dumped on a desert island instead of in the middle of a city. A few uniformed workers scurried for a subway entrance ahead of us. Shadows lurked behind the shop fronts. Otherwise the streets seemed empty.

"Are they all indoors? Watching us? Are we even safe in our own DA?" Karen said the words out loud, but we'd all been thinking them. We walked faster, scurrying past the curtained houses and blank warehouse windows, with the sensation of a thousand eyes boring holes in our backs.

"Steady," said Scylla quietly, when Alden broke into a shambling run. "Almost there. Just around the corner."

We could tell that the first factory was useless without even going in. The windows were shattered and the roof was rusty and probably leaked. We consulted the map and began to walk to the second building.

"Three blocks from a library and only two blocks from a Government food store," Scylla said cheerfully.

"I suppose our credits aren't good anywhere else. I wonder what we do when we need other things?"

"Improvise, I expect. I feel lucky about this place. Being close to things'll be important. No public transport for us."

"I hate walking," snarled Paul, but nobody paid much attention.

We turned the corner and there it was. Built like a for
tress, with bars on the unbroken windows of the second
floor. The key we had been given opened a metal door.
Inside, a huge old-fashioned elevator shook its way up
one floor and opened onto a vast empty space with windows on both sides. Across the cement floor was a tiny
kitchenette and two washrooms, one with a small
shower.

Brad turned on the lights and the stove. Amazingly
they worked. Burning grease smoked up from the old-
fashioned coils of the burner. "I'll clean it tomorrow," he
said, and I knew we had found our new home, even
before he tested the taps and we watched the rusty water
run clean.

It was twilight by the time we'd finished our inspec-
tion. There was a different *feel* about the street below. A
stirring in doorways. Lights coming on. I caught a
glimpse of purple and sequins through a half-curtained
window. It seemed that night was the time for the unemployed and, as we walked back to the center, we saw our
DA beginning to wake up.

"The question is, are they friendly?" Karen asked,
almost matter-of-factly.

"How are we going to find out?" I tried to keep the
wobble out of my voice.

"Carefully. Very carefully. Not by getting beaten up or
ripped off. We should have some ground rules." Brad was
always practical.

"Like what?"

"Never going out alone. Carrying sticks for self-defense."

"Karate," said Katie. "I'll teach any of you who don't know it."

"And that lock on the door is a Mickey-Mouser," Brad added. "We'll need something much more powerful. Electronic keying on the elevator, maybe."

Mindful of the need for security, we asked the receptionist at the rehab center where we could get electronic parts. Her raucous laugh made Brad flush with anger.

"Electronic?" she mocked. "Who do you think you are? You're living rent free. The monthly credits you collect here will buy you food and cleaning supplies and that's it. Damned generous too, if you ask me. It's our taxes you unemployeds are living off, you know."

Trent's freckled face went white and Paul flushed darkly. I knew one or the other would explode and we'd probably all end up sorry for it, so I jumped in, pleading. "There must be ways of getting extra things we need. What about beds and mattresses? Chairs, a table? Cooking things?"

She relented at my meekness. "You scrounge, that's what you do." At our puzzled faces she sighed heavily. "When stores throw out unusable stuff you can take it if you get there before the robot recyclers. And there's nothing to stop you from looking through domestic garbage, if you're not fussy."

For two nights we slept in the rehab center dorms and, during the day, we slaved over our new home. Alden,

Paul, and Trent helped scrub the floors and paint the walls in an off-white color "scrounged" from a paint store because the cans had rusted. On the clean blank surface Scylla began to draw a mural of an elegant courtyard with an iron grille fence and orange trees in tubs. I don't know where she got her ideas. None of us had ever seen any place so exotic. Our warehouse began to look excitingly different.

We deliberately left the windows unwashed—it seemed stupid to signal to the unknown inhabitants of our DA that we had moved in—and we found material for a patchwork assortment of curtains, so that we could hide the light of our room from curious eyes.

And we scrounged. Next to *survival, scrounge* was probably the most important word in our new vocabulary. Brad and Trent, in particular, seemed to have a natural knack for being in the right place at the right time. Beds were hopeless, but they found a store that was throwing out a consignment of water-damaged mattresses. Getting them home was a problem, since we had to make two trips, leaving Brad and Katie, armed with sticks, on guard over the remainder. I truly expected them to be challenged by some gang boss, but they said that the only person who came by was a scrawny little rat of a girl, living alone. We let her have one of the mattresses and I helped her carry it to her billet.

"How long have you been here?" I asked her as we struggled up the stairs to her dingy room. But she just stared at me as if she didn't understand. "From school?"

I added and she grinned. Her teeth were bad and two were missing.

"No school" was all she'd say.

So perhaps there were people even worse off than us, people who'd fallen completely through the cracks and didn't exist as far as the Government was concerned.

Brad found all sorts of electronic parts, thrown out as broken or not up to spec. He came back from one expedition with a black eye, though he made nothing of it. "The shop was close to the boundary of our DA and there was a bit of an argument, that's all."

It scared me to think of Brad braving danger to make life better for the rest of us, and Scylla said we should always go out in groups of three, one to scrounge and two to watch out for the scrounger. And Katie made us work on our karate.

After that we had no more trouble and by the end of a week our home had become our castle, protecting us from the unknown terrors outside. The windows were already barred. The Mickey-Mouse lock had been replaced with a better one, and the elevator was electronically rigged to respond only to our handprints. Any stranger attempting entry would get a sub-lethal shock.

By the end of the first month, when we had to report back to the rehab center for more living credits, our castle was beginning to look quite cozy inside. Screens divided the two sleeping quarters from the rest of the space, and a carpet, hideously designed in mustard and purple, a sagging sofa, four chairs and a bookcase and table, all mended by Brad, made an island of sociability in the sea of concrete floor.

Scylla's studio filled the area opposite the kitchen, living, and bathroom end, with Brad's woodworking bench under the windows. Alden looked at them enviously. "I've got to find something interesting to do or I'll go crazy."

"No one's about to throw out an electronic microscope or a computerized spectroscope, and there's not much you can do without them. I'm in the same boat. There's no future in geology *here*," Katie snapped. Then she sighed and ran a hand through her short hair. "Sorry, Alden. Look, let's explore the library. It may give us some ideas."

That's what it was called: PUBLIC LIBRARY. We weren't sure if we'd be allowed in, but when we got there we realized that there'd be little or no competition. It was a dusty place, with shelves of pre-electronic books, yellowed and mouse-nibbled. The old couple who kept it had long since given up in despair. They hid in their security room, obviously in mortal fear of a gang of unemployed toughs. When they first saw the eight of us, I thought they would have heart attacks then and there. But they became accustomed to us after a while and even gave us advice, through the grille of their door, as to where we might find a particular subject in their eccentric cataloging system.

We were beginning to get used to the idea of never having a job and probably thought about it only a couple of times a day. We were even becoming inured to being pris-

hadn't picked each other for roommates. We had just been put off a bus at the same stop. School was different. Our days had had a shape to them back then, with lectures and labs and assignments. If you couldn't stand a person's mannerisms, you could walk away from them and talk to someone else.

It wasn't so bad for some of us. Scylla painted, whenever she could scrounge materials. Brad was deeply involved in overhauling a discarded electric engine, with an eye to running his woodworking equipment off it. As long as I was somewhere near him I was content. Katie and Karen suffered from boredom, but they at least tried to keep the peace. Alden, Trent, and Paul didn't even try.

"We've got to find something for them to do, something real, not just make-work," Karen said one morning when we'd sent them off to scrounge some chisels for Brad that he didn't really need.

"You're right." Scylla put down her palette and brush and scrubbed her fingers with a paint rag. "Maybe we should take the risk and go out at night. Meet some other people. Some unemployeds. The only faces we ever see are those of the librarians and the woman who runs the food store."

"And she's so like her robots it isn't funny."

"There must be places where people like us meet. Coffee houses or bars."

"It's an awful risk. We're safe in here."

"Lisse, I know. But we can't stay in the womb forever, no matter how cozy. We've got to network. Find another congenial group or two. Maybe they've found ways of keeping their sanity."

Again I remembered: "Enjoy your leisure years. Use them creatively."

I know Scylla and Brad were right, but all the same I was terrified. I remembered feeling sorry for the rats we used to test in mazes in psychology class. I suppose it wasn't that bad a life for them, exploring passages with the reward of a nibble of cheese at the end to keep them on their paws. But what about that horrid moment of looking up, of seeing a great human face, eyes peering down?

Out in the open in the city I felt like that. Afraid of being out there, under the eye of *whoever was in charge.* Like the rats. And I was afraid of the gangs too. We had never seen the nightlife of our DA, but we had certainly heard it, filtering through the barred windows of our castle. The first week or so it had kept us awake. The sounds of raucous laughter. Sometimes screams. The blat-blat of helicopter blades and the sudden searchlight scissoring through the darkness as the thought police descended to quell a riot. I felt that night was a time for locked doors and sleeping with one's head under one's blanket. Yet Scylla was right. We were becoming dangerously ingrown. We had to meet other people, other unemployeds. So out we went, armed with nothing but our wits and our knowledge of karate, to explore the nightlife of our DA and to hear, from strangely different sources, about The Game.

TWO

May to June 2154. Into the Night Jungle

It was a different world. Dingy secondhand shops, which had hidden behind bedraggled net curtains during the day, were transformed into gaudy discos and bars. Where, during the day, the street had been empty except for the occasional worker scurrying from shop to subway, they were now thronged with young people dressed in clothes even more gaudy than ours. They stood in groups under the golden light of the streetlamps. They danced in the middle of the road. They sang, they fought.

We stayed very close together and edged our way down the street, our hands on our credits, looking cautiously over our shoulders, jumping nervously aside when a passerby lurched toward us. After about six blocks the action seemed to die out. Beyond were workers' houses, streets that were empty except for an occasional reveler. We turned back.

"Come on. Let's try this place." Brad led us into a brightly lit room, where we were able to squeeze into a table meant for four, borrowing chairs from neighboring tables.

"Coffee, please," Scylla said to the skinny young man

who wiped our table down with a dirty cloth.

He stared. "There's the house booze," he snapped. "If you're not fussy." He slammed eight glasses down and demanded enough credits to keep us in bread and proteinspread for a week.

"But that's—"

"Pay him, Brad," Scylla whispered, and Brad grudgingly put the money into the outstretched hand.

I sipped my drink and felt my eyes sting and my throat close up. I gasped for air. "Oh, goodness, what *is* this?" I croaked.

Alden took a cautious sip. "Home brew. Heaven knows what it's distilled from, or how, but I wouldn't touch it. It'll certainly numb you, and you might get unlucky and go blind."

"All those credits," moaned Paul. "Whose stupid idea was this anyway?"

I felt like telling him it was his fault, and Alden's and Trent's, that we were going through this instead of being safely and comfortably in our beds, but I managed not to. "Chalk it up to experience," I managed to whisper as my voice came back. "Just look. What a weird group."

"Rather fun." Scylla's eyes sparkled. "Nobody should bother us as long as we have drinks on the table, so let's watch and keep our eyes open."

In this particular place both men and women seemed to have dressed with such extravagance that our bright clothes looked plain and dowdy. There were sequins and feathers, mirrors and jewels, embroidery and gold braid.

Many of the people wore masks, and others had painted their faces in violent denial of their natural shape. One had a third eye painted in the middle of his forehead, another looked like a gorgeous but terrifying parrot.

Music suddenly burst from a loudspeaker in the ceiling and people got up to dance. The floor was tiny, no more than a grudging space between the tables. Shoulder to shoulder they danced, some in pairs, leaning against each other like paired cards in a card house. If one slipped, both would probably fall. Others danced alone, standing in their small space, their eyes fastened on some secret inner world of their own.

The parrot woman was one of these. She spun around, her eyes glazed, and staggered, steadying herself with a hand on Brad's shoulder.

"Cheer up," she said. "You look like a funeral. Was'a matter? C'mon. Be a gen'leman. Buy me a drink."

"Sorry. I think you've had enough, don't you?"

"Enough? You're telling me when I've . . . who are you anyway? Thought p'lice in costume?" She peered owlishly into Brad's face and suddenly snatched the untouched drink from in front of him. She tossed it back as if it were water. Then her eyes, bewildered and hot with anger behind the paint and feathers, glazed over. She sagged bonelessly to the ground.

A garish Pierrot from a nearby table came over. "Sorry. Barb's not usually like this. Disappointed."

"Disappointed in love, you mean?" Scylla asked idly.

The Pierrot laughed. "Who, Barb? No. But she'd

applied to take part in The Game and they turned her down. No surprise to me. I mean, well, *Barb*. They say they always turn you down if you ask anyway. You've got to be invited. I don't put much stock in it either way. What the heck. Eat, drink, and be merry, eh? But Barb was really keen."

Barb stirred. "I feel sick," she muttered, and the Pierrot put his arms under hers and hauled her out before any of us had a chance to ask what The Game was. That's how he had said it. With capital letters. The Game.

Then the disagreeable waiter was back, hovering over our shoulders, telling us to drink up and have another, or leave the table for someone who had more of a thirst. We got up and, as we left the noisy room, I saw him put our glasses on a tray and take them over to some newcomers sitting in the corner. He held out his hand and pocketed the credits. He saw me staring and gave me an impudent grin and winked, as if we were co-conspirators.

We walked home through the gaudy, crowded streets, each of us silent and sad, thinking: is *this* all the world outside has to offer us? In contrast home seemed particularly clean and pleasant. Paul even offered to make us cocoa, and after this soothing drink we went to bed.

Nobody even suggested going out again for a couple of evenings, but on the third night Brad said, "Come on. We'll never find out about our world if we don't take some risks."

This time we stopped outside a small coffee shop called the Purple Orange. Inside were private booths separated by screens of flimsy fabric. An old-fashioned fan in the ceiling turned slowly, making the festoons of fabric quiver and billow. The place looked quiet and sleepy, oddly unreal after the racket outside, and we slid into a booth and asked for tea.

It came on a tray, and with the cups was a small box containing eight buff-colored cigarettes. The waiter mentioned the price, which would just about have paid our month's food bills.

"We don't smoke," Scylla said firmly.

I poured tea and we sipped and looked around. It was obvious that this was not going to be a good place to meet new people. In spite of the soft background music it was almost unnaturally quiet, and we found ourselves whispering uneasily. In the shadows of the other booths pale faces gleamed. They weren't talking together, not even looking around, just staring into space with vacant smiles. It gave me the shivers and I said so.

"Agreed, Lisse. There's something odd about this place."

"Mind-altering drugs," Alden said knowledgeably. "If the thought police should get on to them . . ."

As we got to our feet, a large man slipped ahead of us and lounged against the door. "Going so soon? Don't you like our place?"

"Not particularly," said Brad levelly. "It's not quite what we expected."

"Oh? Just what *were* you expecting?"

"I'm not sure. I'll tell you when we find it. Now, if

you'll excuse us . . ." As he moved forward, the man moved, too, and suddenly Brad was flat on his back on the floor.

I screamed. It was stupid, but I just couldn't help it. For a horrible instant I thought Brad was dead.

"Now, listen, you." The man put his'foot on Brad's chest. Brad gasped. "We go to a lot of trouble to have this place nice for our customers. We don't expect people to waltz in, have a cup of tea, and waltz out again. That doesn't even cover our expenses."

"Sorry. There was nothing we liked. Brad, are you all right?" Katie bent down. There was a sudden grunt and now it was the fat man who was lying on the floor. Brad scrambled up and we stepped over the hustler and got out fast.

"A few more karate lessons before we venture out again, I think." Katie's voice was just a little unsteady as we headed home, not exactly at a run but walking very briskly.

For the next few weeks we practiced karate twice a day. It was fun, it passed the time, and Alden, Trent, and Paul took out their aggressions on the mat, so there was no more bickering. In between practice sessions we sold some of Scylla's paintings outside the subway station, getting enough credits for a couple of nights out.

"Shall we try again? I'm ready to take on anyone," Alden said one day after three successful bouts on the karate mat.

"Yes, let's. I want to find out more about this 'Game.'"

"Me too. What can it be? Why was that parrot girl so upset? It's driving me crazy guessing."

"We can't let you go crazy, Lisse. All right, everyone?" Brad looked around. We all nodded and, ready for anything but with a wary anticipation, we went out that night.

It was a bit of an anticlimax, after psyching ourselves up and all those karate lessons, to find the Coffee Bush. It had cheerful orange curtains in the windows; the tables and the floor were not just clean, they shone. Green plants hung from the ceiling in polished brass bowls. As for the clientele, they looked . . . well, normal. Like us. We found a free table and ordered synthespresso.

There was a low hum of conversation in the background, the occasional amused laugh. It was warm and bright, but not too bright. We grinned at each other and ordered seconds.

A burly man, dressed as inconspicuously as Brad, strolled over, mug in hand. "May I join you?"

"Of course. Pull up a chair."

We all moved over to give him room and introduced ourselves. He said his name was Charlie and that he'd been out of school and unemployed for a year. That surprised me. He seemed to me to be a whole lot older than that, but perhaps one aged fast in the city. It always seemed odd to me that our life expectancy should go *down* when there was no poverty and no tension about having to earn a living. Maybe boredom was aging.

I came out of my daydream to find that Charlie had

made the others so comfortable they were sharing with him our experiences in the city and our feelings about the nightlife.

". . . and psychedels of every kind," Alden was just saying. "I can't imagine where they get them."

"Make them, I suppose." Charlie shrugged.

"That's impossible. You'd need . . ." Alden reeled off a mind-numbing list of chemicals. "Not to mention an up-to-date lab and a lot of know-how. Some of that stuff is pretty dangerous if you're not careful."

"You know a lot about it."

"I'm a chemist. I mean I *would* have been a chemist." Alden's face closed and he got that sullen look. Darn, I thought. Just when everything was going so well. I hoped Charlie wouldn't say anything stupid or tactless.

He didn't. He just nodded and changed the subject. The owner produced trays of hot appetizers, delicious stuff, and we drank more coffee.

"Charlie, what's The Game?" I had suddenly remembered.

He swung around and stared at me, his face suddenly hard. No friendly smile. "What d'you mean? There's no game. I was on my own this evening and I thought you looked like good company."

I laughed. "I didn't mean what was *your* game." And I explained what the Pierrot had said.

"Ah!" Charlie stroked his chin and then looked at his watch. "The Game. With capital letters. Look, it's getting late and I have to get home. Why don't we meet here tomorrow and I'll tell you what I know, which isn't much."

We talked among ourselves—did we have enough credits for another night out?—and agreed to meet at the Coffee Bush at ten the next evening. We shook hands all around, very friendly. But as we walked home I had the odd feeling that he was playing for time, that he knew perfectly well what The Game was, but wasn't sure if he wanted to tell us. Or—I thought this later, as I wrote up the night's events in my journal before falling into bed— perhaps he'd never *heard* of The Game but didn't want to appear ignorant. Either way, it would be interesting to hear what he had to say. But I wasn't at all sure I trusted Charlie.

The next evening he was waiting for us, and a tray with eight steaming mugs of synthespresso was put on the table before we'd had a chance to order. Brad held out a couple of credits but Charlie pushed his hand away. "On the house."

"Is this *your* place, then?" Karen asked after we'd thanked him.

"I have an interest in it," Charlie said modestly. Again I wondered if he really was only a year older than we were. He'd come a long way in a year, if so.

"The Game," I reminded him. "You were going to tell us about it."

"Something for something." He smiled as if it were a joke, but I could feel the hard edge under his friendliness. I realized he was a person who wouldn't give *anything* away, except a cup of coffee to soften up a client.

"We've got nothing useful to trade," Katie said, bewildered.

"What had you in mind?" Scylla asked at the same time.

"Information. I was particularly interested in your background in chemistry." He had turned to Alden. "We could be very useful to each other."

"Oh? I don't see how. It wasn't good enough to get me a job. I don't see what possible use it might be to you." Alden looked bleaker and more beaky than usual, like a starving eagle.

"That's because you don't think like an entrepreneur. You're still thinking in old patterns—a government job or nothing. It's ridiculous how many people give up at that stage. What you've got to understand is that there are thousands and thousands of young unemployeds in this city alone, all of them with needs. So just ask yourselves, what are those needs?"

He paused dramatically and looked at us one by one, starting with Brad, who was sitting on his left, and finishing with me. "Come on, Lisse. You sit very quietly and watch and listen. What do you make of it all? What do you think people are looking for?"

"Happiness," I answered without thinking. The word fell off my tongue as if he'd willed me to say it.

"Happiness." Charlie's voice was soft, persuasive. "Right on the mark. It'd be worth a fortune, wouldn't it? To guarantee happiness."

"But you can't!" I burst out. "Happiness isn't a goal, it's a result. If you've got a job that's worth doing. If you can be proud of yourself. If people respect and care for you, and you for them. You can't buy *that*."

"Charlie's talking about chemical happiness, aren't you, Charlie?" Alden cut in dryly. "Pills or cigarettes. Like we saw in the Purple Orange."

"Not at all. You're way off base, Alden, my friend. What I have in mind is infinitely safer and more sophisticated than the garbage the Purple Orange dishes out."

"You're still talking illegal substances, aren't you?"

"And you're talking like you got out of school yesterday."

"Charlie," interrupted Karen, "why don't you give Alden a chance to think about it? I believe you've taken his breath away with your proposition. We'd like a chance to talk it over privately. Meanwhile, let's have another coffee, and *you* tell us what you know about The Game."

Clever Karen, I thought.

Charlie stared at her. Karen looked back, her blue eyes frank, untroubled. "I've been curious ever since we came across the phrase *The Game*. You've been around. You must know what's going on, better than most."

"That's true enough. But you'll be disappointed. It's boring stuff compared with what I have to offer. It's just a propaganda tool of the thought police to keep the unemployed masses amused, that's all."

"Like the ancient Romans, you mean?" Karen said. "They gave the plebs free bread and beer and entertained them with circuses so they wouldn't revolt."

Brad leaned forward. "We're already getting the free bread and beer, more or less, but what about this circus? Is that what it is? If so, why isn't it advertised? Why haven't we been told?"

"That's their cunning. Psychological, you see. They make it difficult for you to take part in it. Even finding out what's going on isn't easy. So if you *do* get into it, you feel you've won. You're ahead of the rest, see? Like I said, psychological."

"But what actually *is* it?"

"Some kind of treasure hunt. You go to a special place and get clues to help you look for something. Once you've found it, you move on to another level and—"

"Like a stupid video game?" Brad's voice was disgusted. He'd cracked every game at school in his first three years.

"No, not a bit. This is real. At least, that's what they say."

"How can we join? Where is it?"

Charlie shrugged. "Dunno. I haven't got involved myself. Too busy making money, wrapping up this DA. But I'll tell you one thing. It's not here. You have to get to it by train."

"Then it's useless, isn't it?" Paul sounded really disappointed. I hadn't thought he'd care that much. "We've got no travel permits. We can't get out of our DA."

Charlie laughed. "Babes in the wood, that's what your bunch is. You need Charlie's helping hand. Tell you what, if you think seriously about coming in with me,

Alden, I'll see that you all get your travel permits."

We stared at him. *Travel* permits? Who was this Charlie to have that kind of power?

Alden looked more like a hungry eagle than ever. "Have you got a lab?"

"Best that money can buy."

"Computer? This is complex stuff. You need—"

He stopped as the smile on Charlie's face widened. He nodded and we stared incredulously at one another. No unemployed person had access to a computer. That was axiomatic. Computers were information. Information was power. No government would leave that kind of power in the hands of the unemployed, we knew that. This was why we lived close to the library, why we had to read bound books. The past we were permitted. It was only from the future that we were cut off.

And Charlie had access to the future.

Be careful, Alden. I wanted to yell it out loud. This Charlie must be at least twenty-five years old, maybe older. And he had enough power to ruin us if we didn't do what he wanted.

"Very interesting." Alden got to his feet and held out his hand, smiling. "I'll think it over and let you know."

"You do that."

"No hard feelings if I decide against your proposition?"

"I never waste time on hard feelings, Alden, my boy. I leave the *feeling* to the other guy."

We got out of the café and hurried down the road. It

was still quite dark and there was no moon. The lights made islands of orange in the dark sea of the street. Their glare blurred out the sky.

"Well, that was the weirdest—"

"Hush, Katie. Not till we get home." Alden's face looked even more like a hungry eagle in the unnatural glare of the lights.

"This way, I think." Brad suddenly dodged down a side street and led us along a labyrinthine route that eventually got us to the warehouse. He unlocked the door and pushed us inside. Then he stood with the door barely ajar, listening. Finally he eased it shut and turned the key in the lock.

"What was that all about?" Karen was laughing.

"I don't *think* we were followed—"

"Oh, come on!"

"If Charlie's all that powerful, he probably already knows everything about this place down to the color of the walls." Trent's voice was dry.

I shivered. "You won't go back there, will you, Alden? He'll kill you if you say no to his scheme."

"What makes you so sure I won't say yes?" His eyes gleamed in the dim light of the hallway.

"Alden, you wouldn't . . ."

"It'd be so good to be in a decent research facility." He sighed. "But of course I won't. I'll just say no."

"But he'll . . ."

"I think you're exaggerating my importance to him. There must be plenty of would-be chemists out there. If I refuse him politely he'll just shrug it off and look for another person."

"Or he could break your legs. I don't like what he said about leaving the *feeling* to the other person."

"You won't go alone, that's for sure, Alden." Brad was definite.

Sparked with caffeine and with the uncomfortable feeling that perhaps our castle was not as secure as we had believed it to be, none of us slept very well. When I struggled up from a nightmarish sleep it was almost noon. Paul and Scylla were cooking breakfast. Trent and Brad were at his work table, deep in conversation.

"Good morning. What are you up to?"

"Our castle has a moat and a drawbridge. Now we're planning to add a portcullis."

"What's a portcullis?" I yawned till my jaw cracked.

"A kind of raised gate with spikes on it. If the enemy got across the moat and entered the gatehouse, then they dropped this thing on them," Karen explained.

"Only *this* spiky trap will be an electric charge on our front door."

"How will we be able to get in and out?"

"I'd like it to be voice controlled if I can scrounge a decent microphone and some other bits and pieces. We should have a different phrase for each of us to say, to make doubly sure."

I shivered and pushed my hands into my pockets. "You really do believe he might try to break Alden's legs?"

"I don't think he'd stop with Alden. After all, why should he?"

"I wish we'd never discovered the Coffee Bush!"

"I wish we'd never discovered Charlie. Too bad about the café. That was fantastic espresso. You'd swear it was made with real beans." Scylla sighed dramatically. "I wish we had enough credits to buy decent coffee. Come on, children, breakfast's ready."

In the afternoon we went searching for bits and pieces for Brad's portcullis. Although we weren't allowed to buy anything, people sometimes threw away old radios and other things we could cannibalize. We also stocked up on food, using our last credits for the month. "In case of siege," Scylla said, but I *think* she was joking.

We passed right outside the Coffee Bush. By day it looked like a shabby rooming house with dirty lace curtains and a rubber plant in the window. "A perfect disguise. You would never guess what it was at night," Brad remarked, almost admiringly.

"I think it's scary." I found myself shivering although the day was warm. "What's behind *this* window, do you suppose? Or *that* one over there?"

"How important *is* Charlie? Maybe this whole area is his," Karen put in.

"Or maybe he's a small-time thug, just scaring us for the fun of it, with nothing to back him up."

"That's the comforting thought for the day." Alden cracked a smile. He'd been very quiet during our expedition.

"Thank goodness, we're almost home." I'd been feeling nervous prickles running down my spine for the last half hour, as if some invisible person had been watching.

The person in charge of the rat maze, maybe.

Brad unlocked the outside door and stared at the metal frame. "Scratched," he said briefly, when we asked what was the matter. "Someone's been trying to get in. But not very efficiently."

"So they *do* know where we live."

"Who do you mean—*they?*"

"Charlie and his friends." Brad locked the main door behind us. "We'd better get that portcullis rigged."

It took Trent and Brad three days to work on the bits and pieces we'd found and put together a voice-activated door lock. Each of us had to speak a phrase into the microphone: I chose "open sesame" although I was almost past joking.

"I can go alone," Alden said on the third night. "No need to involve the rest of you."

"Don't be crazy. We stick together. All or none."

"We have the advantage," Katie reminded us. "He thinks we're innocent and ignorant. He's going to rely on brute force. Low cunning will take him by surprise. If you remember all the karate I've taught you and if we plan a strategy ahead of time, I think we've got a good chance, no matter how many thugs Charlie brings along."

"You don't think it'll just be Charlie?"

"Didn't you see his hands? Soft as a baby's. No lumps or scars. Charlie has other people to do his fighting for him. You can count on that."

We set out for the Coffee Bush later than before. We wanted to make sure that the café was full. Charlie wouldn't disturb his regulars by having Alden beaten up on the premises, we reckoned, so we felt fairly comfort-able letting him go in alone, while we lurked in the shad-ows between streetlamps a little way down the block.

Around us swirled the city's nightlife, people drunk, zombied out of their minds, people fighting, making love. Sounds of weeping and of raucous laughter. And every-where the purple, yellow, green, shocking pink, feathers, sequins, satins of the unemployed.

How long Alden was taking! Had we made a fatal error in thinking Charlie wouldn't do anything violent in his own place? Had Alden's body been thrown out on the rubbish heap in some squalid alley behind the building?

"Let's go in. Let's find him," I whispered.

Brad put a hand on my arm. "It's all right. Here he comes now."

Alden's face had its usual eagle look, perhaps a bit paler than usual, but he was whistling and I knew he'd enjoyed saying no to Charlie.

He was about thirty feet away when the street seemed to explode. I couldn't see where they all came from, it was so quick. Out of doorways, I suppose, dropping off roofs. But suddenly Alden had collapsed under a pile of bodies and we sprinted into action.

We had surprise as well as craft on our side. Charlie's soldiers were thugs, big, brutal, slow-thinking. No match for our karate. We got through to Alden as fast as we could and hauled him to his feet, then turned to face the opposition. We hadn't had time to get in more than a few good kicks before the helicopter dropped down and starting spraying stun smoke.

I stumbled as a whiff of the bitter stuff made my head spin, but Katie caught me by the arm as I staggered. In another minute, as we sprinted down the street, I was all right. Brad had thrown Alden over his shoulder and was keeping up with the rest of us, stride for stride. As we turned the corner, I saw Charlie's men, like a heap of rag dolls, being hauled into the helicopter.

"How d'you feel?" Brad asked, as we lowered Alden into the softest of our sagging chairs.

"I'll live." Alden tried to sit up and collapsed with a grunt of pain. His hand felt his cheekbone, where a swelling was already turning blue.

"I think some ribs are cracked." Scylla knelt beside him, her fingers exploring his right side. Alden winced at her touch. "I'll bandage them tightly and hope nothing's badly broken. I wish I knew more about medicine."

"Should have had old Rich here," Karen joked.

"I'd rather have broken ribs," Alden retorted. "And for goodness sake don't make me laugh. It's killing me."

"You *were* brave. What did Charlie do when you said no?" I asked.

Alden shrugged and flinched. "Just shook my hand and said he hoped I wouldn't regret it."

"D'you think he'll keep after us?"

"Hard to say, Lisse. It was a bit of luck, the police helicopter coming just then. If those thugs of Charlie's have any instincts of self-preservation they'll never tell him we won. They'll tell him they beat the daylights out of us before the police arrived, and that'll be the end of it."

"I think it all went very well." Brad grinned.

"Thanks to all of you." Alden flushed. "It was my fault for sounding off about my knowledge, as if it mattered."

"Nonsense. 'One for all and all for one,'" quoted Karen.

"That's a great motto. Let's drink to it." So we had a cup of cocoa and went to bed.

The motto did seem to express something that had happened to us as we fought Charlie's thugs. Before that night we'd been eight friends from school who, for practical reasons, had decided to share a home. After the fight we were a family, a unit that nothing and no one could separate. Something else had happened, something personal I couldn't share with the others. When Brad had put his hand on my arm I hadn't felt a thing, not a tingle. It's as if, without my noticing when or how, he'd turned from the special someone I dreamed about into a brother. It was sad in a way, but it had always been a one-sided dream. He'd never thought of me as anything but a friend. As I curled up in bed, watching the dawn filter through the filthy factory windows, I told myself that I was better off. Now I had four brothers and three sisters, instead of a hopeless love.

It was four days before Alden could walk far without pain. But once the bruises began to yellow he got restless.

"You don't want another taste of nightlife, do you?"

"Good grief, no. But what about The Game?"

There was a moment's silence.

"I'd forgotten . . ."

"Charlie didn't tell us much . . ."

"Sounded like fun, though. A treasure hunt . . ."

"But it's not in our DA. You have to get there by train."

That threw cold water on our enthusiasm, but only for a while. Later that day Brad suddenly said, "Charlie can't be the only person with connections. Perhaps you *can* get train tickets if you know who to ask."

"But who? And where would we find them? At night clubs?"

We groaned, back full circle.

"There's no law against going down into the subway and looking around, is there? Maybe there's a poster. Or we could ask a robot," I suggested.

To be doing anything, however feeble, was better than doing nothing. We set out at once for the nearby subway station where we sold Scylla's paintings when we needed extra credits. We hit a time when the workers were changing shift, and the usually deserted streets were thronged with soberly clad people, many of them carrying briefcases and lunchboxes. We followed them down the stairs, feeling out of place in our garish clothes, like kingfishers in a flock of starlings. Would we be thrown out?

I had never been in a station in my life and I had no idea what to expect. The novels I had read led me to imagine a dingy place, filled with soot and belching smoke, but of course that was long ago when there were fossil fuels. This place had shining tiled walls and a floor that was constantly kept clean by a janitor-robot.

The workers ignored us, intent on racing down the branching passages toward the trains, whose distant thunder we could hear. Each of them slipped a card into a turnstile slot, retrieved it, and pushed through.

"Permanent passes to work," Scylla guessed.

"But there must be times when they want to buy a single ticket to go to somewhere else. I wonder how they do that?"

We looked about us. On one wall was a large illustrated map of the system, illuminated in different colors, the same colors, I noticed, that marked the entrances to the different passages. A simple code to follow, once one had crossed the hurdle of the turnstile. As we stared at the map, a woman in sober work clothes touched a station on the map, put a coin in a slot, and received a ticket in return.

As she turned away with a suspicious and disapproving look at us, we pushed Brad after her. "Go on, ask her."

The woman laughed, and I saw Brad turn red.

"What did you say to her?" we asked him when she had gone.

"I asked which train to take to The Game."

"What did she say?"

"Just that games were for children and that she was an adult, thank you very much. Made me feel like an idiot. Someone else can ask next time."

"I don't see what's to stop us from jumping the turnstile. It's not very high. There's no one around. How would they ever know?"

"It's illegal. And they'd be bound to find out."

"It might be worth the risk if we knew where to go. But where *is* The Game?"

We were still standing by the map, looking at the names, wondering if one of them might be a clue, when a sudden commotion made us turn. For a horrible moment I thought it might be Charlie's thugs again. Down here it would be more difficult to take them by surprise.

But it wasn't Charlie's thugs. It was the thought police. I recognized the uniform at once. They were holding a very small man between them. He wasn't young, and he was dressed in a gray jumpsuit that was obviously far too large for him, though I suppose he had picked it because of its inconspicuous color. His lips were drawn back in a desperate grimace so that his teeth gleamed in the light, and his eyes were rolled back in his head so that I could see their whites.

The thought police, in their navy-and-silver uniforms, strode smoothly along the corridor toward us, the little gray man between them. I was surprised that he could keep up with them. Then, as they passed, I could see that the little man's feet weren't touching the floor at all. They went up the stairs together, all three, and his toes went flop, flop, against the metal edge of each stair.

A few people, who must have got off the same train, followed at a discreet distance, each of them looking straight ahead, ignoring the unpleasantness. Impulsively, I stepped forward and stopped one of them.

"Please, what did he do?"

The man stared at me as if I were an alien. I thought he was going to push right past me, but then he spoke grudgingly. "I tried to ride the train without a ticket, of course."

"But how did they *know*?" I asked stupidly.

"The computer tracks every passenger. If the people and the tickets don't match, it notifies the authorities. Nobody but a fool would try to cheat the transit system. A fool or an unemployed." He glared at me, spitting out the words.

"Thank you, sir. Of course I wouldn't . . ." But with an impatient snort he ran up the stairs, leaving me burbling foolishly.

On the way back home I told the others what the man had said. "That's it then," said Brad gloomily. He was really taken with the idea of The Game.

"We mustn't give up yet. We can ask the librarians."

"Or go back to the rehab center. That woman might know . . ."

Next day we went to the library, but the only lead the librarians could give us took us to books on games for children, a book called *Games People Play*, another called *Famous End Games*, and half a dozen on games theory. When we went to the rehab center, the receptionist stared at us coldly. "It's not your day for credits."

We tried to explain, but her face was as blank as a closed door. "Sorry. Don't know what you're talking about."

We went home feeling really depressed. It was stupid. If we'd never heard about The Game we'd be happily doing all the things that had kept us busy before. But now it was different. Trent and Paul started bickering again and even Scylla didn't have her usual zest.

On our way back from the library two days later, Brad unlocked the warehouse door, as usual with a swift look up and down the street to make sure no one was in sight. As he closed it behind us, Karen put her palm on the elevator lock. We pulled the rickety doors open and stepped in.

"Hello. What's this?" Alden bent down with a grunt—I guess his ribs still hurt—and picked up a large manila envelope. There was nothing on the outside to indicate who it was for, nothing but the muddy footprint Alden had just put there.

"How did it get there? The outside door was locked."

"Easy enough to force, I suppose. We saw scratches before, remember?"

"But not the elevator."

"Maybe whoever put it there poked it through the grillework." The elevator door had metal strips that crossed each other and slid together as the door opened.

"Let's get inside. This is scary. I'm going to change that outside lock first thing."

He pushed the button and the elevator creaked its way upward. We neutralized the portcullis and crowded through the door into the security of our home.

"Has anyone been in here?"

"I don't see how they could."

"Better look around, though."

It was only after we had looked in every cranny of our home that we remembered the envelope and gathered, still feeling jittery, around Alden. He tore it open and drew out eight smaller white envelopes, each of which had a name on it. "Scylla, Brad, Katie, Paul, Trent, Karen. One for me. And this is yours, Lisse."

I stared at the black typing on the envelope and slowly tore it open. What could it be? Inside was a plastic token, like the ones we had seen the workers use to get through the subway station turnstile. And an oblong card. Upon the card, in formal italic script, was printed:

You are cordially invited
to participate in The Game
Date: 17.06.2154
Time: 1430
Place: Barton Oaks

THREE

17 June, 2154. Bread and Circuses

An invitation to The Game! Where had it come from? Who, apart from the librarians and those horrible people we had met during our dip into the night jungle of our DA, knew of our curiosity? The receptionist at the center. Could it be her? It was a fruitless question but still we kept asking it, as the hours passed, incredibly slowly, until it was time to leave for the train station.

As we left the safety of our warehouse home, I almost wished that the invitation had never come. My palms were sweaty and I rubbed them on the sides of my cherry-red jumpsuit. *Scaredy-cat,* I told myself and looked shamefacedly at the others. I felt better when I saw that Alden's face was paler than usual and that Karen's usually cheerful face was grave.

"Here goes." Brad locked the outer door behind us. "Come on."

We marched with a kind of artificial confidence along the street and down the subway stairs, clutching our plastic tokens. We looked at the map and found that Barton Oaks was at the extreme northern end of the purple line. We pushed our tokens into the slots and the turnstile admitted us to the passages beyond.

My heart was thudding as we followed the purple markers down a moving staircase, along another passage, down another set of stairs, until we reached two platforms, with arrows marked "north" and "south." So far so good. We looked at each other, our feelings a mixture of excitement and fear.

A few workers stood on the northbound platform. They eyed us suspiciously, as if we had no right to be there, and I found myself playing with my token, casually, but so they could see it. I didn't want them to be tempted to call the thought police.

"Are we sure we're in the right place?" Katie asked anxiously.

"Brad, go and ask."

"Why me?" But he went over to a waiting group.

"Can't you read?" I could hear the sarcastic voice of the worker above the rushing sound of the circulating air. He pointed to an illuminated sign: "Train one, local to . . ." followed by a list of names.

"That's not much help," Brad snapped back. At that moment the list reeled up to the top and a new sign followed: "Train two, limited express to Barton Oaks."

"Train two. Thanks a lot." Brad turned on his heel and walked back to our group, his face flushed.

"To think our taxes go to support that spoiled bunch of layabouts." The man spoke to the tiled wall that curved up to the round ceiling across the track.

"'Tisn't right, is it?" A woman chimed in. She shot a look of dislike at us. "Just look at them! What a useless . . ."

Trent started forward, but Scylla caught his arm. "It's not worth it," she said softly. "Don't start anything now. If we miss our chance we might never get another." I'm sure that if she hadn't kept a friendly grip on his arm he would have flung himself on the disagreeable worker and given him a going-over that would have landed him in jail—or the psych ward. I remembered stories that had been whispered in school. And I remembered the terror on the face of the gray man being dragged from the subway by the thought police.

A sudden roar drowned out the worker's obnoxious remarks. We all turned in alarm toward the sound, in time to see something like a metal capsule shoot from the round tunnel at the end of the platform and screech to a stop. Doors slid open. The workers climbed aboard and the doors shut. The capsule screamed off to the right, leaving behind a strange smell of burnt dust and ozone. We were alone on the platform. We looked at each other and grinned feebly. So that was a train!

Ours arrived about five minutes later. We leapt aboard, afraid of being left behind. The doors slid shut and we found seats. My heart was pounding, and I felt almost sick with excitement. This was a real *train*. I had read about them, of course, and seen old-fashioned ones in videos at school, but to *ride* in one was almost more than I could bear.

After a moment or two I realized that we were actually traveling *under* the city. Already we must have left our Designated Area and were beneath alien territory. It was an extraordinarily scary idea.

I stared out of the window at blackness, interrupted by an occasional flash of light, in which I could see shadowy pipes along the walls surrounding our capsule. There was no sensation of speed. It was only when we slowed to approach a station that any sense of motion returned in the quick flicker of signs passing outside the window.

We stopped twice, once to let on a group of six workers in black uniforms with silver braid and buttons, who looked at us ferociously but fortunately left us alone. The second group to board the train were unemployeds, like us. I looked at them with interest, wondering if they might be from our school, but they were strangers. And perhaps enemies. After all, they came from a different Designated Area. I risked a smile at the girl sitting across the aisle from me.

"Are you going to Barton Oaks as well?" I asked her.

She nodded and smiled back. "It's your first time, isn't it?"

"Yes. What's it like? What do we do?"

She shook her head. "They'll explain when you get there. Nothing I could say would be useful. Each group's experience is unique. And private." Her voice was low, so I had to lean forward to catch her words.

I flushed and drew back. "I'm sorry. I didn't know."

"That's all right. You'll learn. Have you been out of school long?" She didn't say how young we looked, but I could read her expression.

"Two months."

Her eyebrows went up. "Really? That's a short time. We weren't invited till our group was over a year old. But then we'd had problems with a couple who couldn't fit in."

"What has one's group got to do with—? Sorry, I forgot."

I stared out at the blackness rushing by. How long was this journey? How far had we come? I had a million questions. Then I felt the pressure against my body as we slowed down. There were flashes of light in the darkness outside. A white-tiled platform slid into view. It was identical to the one we had left, except that this one had the words BARTON OAKS in purple tiles on the white walls.

We followed the old-timers up the stairs and along a passage. Then, instead of following the workers upstairs, they turned down another passage that ended in a blank wall.

I watched carefully as the other group inserted their tokens in a slot in the wall. A door slid open.

"Good luck." My train companion smiled as they walked through into the darkness beyond.

I stepped impulsively forward, but the door slid shut in my face. There was nothing but a blank wall.

"Insert your tokens in—" a robot voice stated, but I was ahead of it, pushing my token into the slot. The others did the same and once more the door opened and we crowded inside.

What had I expected? Something bright and garish, I think, like a video arcade. Certainly not a soft gray carpet, translucent walls whose color trembled and changed as I looked at them. There was a faint flowery scent in the air. No sign of the old-timers.

We walked slowly forward. The passage widened into a kind of anteroom, empty except for a vase of real flowers on a low table. They were waxy white and their scent permeated the air. It was quiet and warm, like . . . no, nothing in my whole life offered me any comparison.

I think we all jumped when the robot appeared, soft-footed, in the doorway. It seemed very out of place amid this elegance.

"Follow me, please."

Brad, Trent, Alden, and Paul were shown one room and we women were taken to another. For a moment I panicked. What was going to happen? Why were they breaking us up? "Scylla, shouldn't we stick together?"

"It's all right, Lisse. Look, they're changing rooms."

We stepped out of our street clothes and replaced them with the coveralls and boots that lay neatly on shelves at the far end of the room. There was every possible size to choose from, but otherwise they were an identical greenish-gray.

A human male was waiting for us in the anteroom. "The group from DA Forty-three, I believe? How do you do. I am the Game Manager."

He shook hands with each of us in turn and then led us to another room, even quieter and grayer and softer-feeling than the one from which we had come. It was furnished with nothing but a dozen reclining chairs, placed in rows.

"Sit down. Get comfortable. I'm going to explain what all this is about. I'm sure you're very curious." He perched on one of the chairs, swinging his legs. "I understand that one of your group is a historian—Karen, isn't it? So you may already have some idea of societal games of the past."

"Bread and circuses," I blurted out and blushed, feeling it was rather a rude comment on our Government, comparing it with the cynical attitude of the Roman authorities toward the common people.

Luckily he took it in good part and smiled. "A more useful comparison might be the war games of the late twentieth century. The people back in those days were highly competitive and warlike. In spite of being fully employed, they still had aggressive impulses that had to be channeled into physical contact sports and later into video games and, ultimately, into the live war game.

"The participants in war games dressed in coveralls, were armed with rifles or handguns loaded with dye, and then proceeded to hunt one another through a wilderness terrain. The game was later refined by having participants wear heat-sensitive uniforms and use low-energy laser weapons, each strike registering as a colored patch on the uniform. Some of these games took several days, with teams working together, or challenges might be set up between champions.

"Of course, no one in today's society would want to participate in such a violent ego-centered competition. The Game, as we have refined it to suit the needs of today, is a *cooperative* venture, during which the participants will hunt for clues."

"Then it *is* a treasure hunt!"

"But what kind of treasure?"

The Game Manager smiled. "The treasure will be ultimately defined as the fulfilling of your common need. Naturally it differs somewhat for every group."

"Are you saying that if we win we'll get our heart's desire? How can we possibly? I mean . . . I don't even know what my heart's desire *is*."

"That is a little too complex to explain at this time. Perhaps in working together cooperatively during your searches you will discover what it *is* you really need and desire."

"Searches? Plural? Does The Game go on for a long time, then?"

"It differs in length, depending on many factors, among them the skill and quality of cooperation within the group."

Paul got to his feet. "I don't know about the rest of you, but I feel we know all we need to know. When can we get started and see for ourselves what it's all about?"

The Game Manager quelled his upward movement with a gesture. "One moment, please. It is necessary to get into the mood, as it were. If you will just relax in your chairs and close your eyes . . ."

Even as I leaned back obediently, feeling the chair unfold beneath me, supporting my back and legs, I felt a twinge of disappointment. So it's not really going to happen at all, I thought, as I closed my eyes. It's just hypnosis. A glorified dream.

The Game Manager must have switched on a sunlamp.

I could feel its heat on my face and I could see a glow through my closed eyelids. I knew what hypnosis was like, of course. It had been one of the many adjustment techniques used in school. I remembered the weightless sensation, as if my body had been floating in a black velvet space.

Funny. It wasn't like that now. The chair pressed hard against my spine. The light beat relentlessly against my closed eyelids. I felt very much awake. It isn't going to work, I thought. I remembered old techniques, let my hands drop to my sides and tried consciously to relax.

My fingertips curled and felt something gritty. That was ridiculous. The chair on which I was reclining was covered in soft gray cloth. I flattened my hand against the surface and flexed my fingers. They closed on a handful of sand. Hot, dry sand. I sat up, opened my eyes, and cried out, "Oh, look!"

Around me, the others stirred and sat up. We seemed to be in the middle of a desert. Brown sand stretched to a horizon of blue in every direction, except to our left, where the emptiness was interrupted by a high flat-topped rock rising abruptly, like a reddish cylinder, from the sand. Overhead a couple of large birds flapped and soared lazily in a current of warm air. Apart from the birds and the eight of us, no living thing stirred.

How quiet it was. Had I gone deaf? I swallowed and the silence pressed against my ears like hot cloth. How empty. A space so uncrowded that one could strain one's ears for five minutes and not hear a thing, could stretch one's eyes to the horizon and not see a single dwelling, a solitary person.

"It can't be real!" I gasped.

"Of course not. It's a typical hypnotic scenario." Trent was definite.

"So what happens next?"

"I suppose we wait and see what happens."

We basked in the sunshine. Overhead the birds circled lazily. The sand stretched emptily to the horizon. The silence was unbroken.

"Well, nothing's going to happen unless we make it." Brad sprang to his feet at last and brushed the sand off his hands. "And if we're to find clues we'd better start looking."

"But where?" I asked. "How will we know a clue when we see one?"

"Something that sticks out, something out of the ordinary."

Karen laughed. "There's only one thing sticking out." She pointed at the mesa. "I wonder if it's climbable? You'd get a spectacular view from the top."

We set off, four walking around the rock to the left, four to the right, looking for ledges, crevices, anything that might be a useful toehold. Almost halfway around, out team found a rounded channel, like an exposed volcanic vent, which meandered up the side of the rock. We couldn't see if it went clear to the top, but it looked possible.

We called to the others and, when they had joined us,

we worked out a plan of action. It wasn't going to be easy climbing without ropes. We had been exposed to adventure experiences at school, so we'd done some mountaineering, but this volcanic plug was totally different from the grass-topped crags we were accustomed to.

Katie, Trent, and Brad were the best climbers. I was nimble, but I was small and didn't have the reach of the others. We set out with Katie in the lead, followed by Paul, Trent, Scylla, Alden, Brad, me, and Karen.

The sun glanced across the fissure we were to climb, so that every toe- and fingerhold was etched in shadow. This was a plus. On the negative side, at times the sun shone full in our faces, almost blinding us.

We spoke very little as we climbed, just a terse word to indicate a toehold. There was a nasty moment when I tried to get a grip on a narrow ridge just beyond my reach. My fingers slipped and pain shot up my arm as the skin tore on the razor-sharp edge of the rock. My left foot slipped and I screamed.

"It's all right. I've got you." I could feel Karen's hand firmly pushing my foot back onto the narrow ledge.

I reached up again, straining for a fingerhold, but my fingertips were slippery with fresh blood. "I can't . . ."

Brad caught my wrist and he and Karen boosted me up to the next ledge. From then on the climb was straightforward, a set of nearly parallel ledges like an eccentric staircase.

One by one, we rolled over the top and lay panting in the clean dry air. There was a thin layer of soil covered with short dry grass and a creeping herb, which gave off a delightfully pungent smell when crushed. Katie said she'd never seen anything like it before. She tugged at its tough stem and managed to break off a specimen to stow safely in one of the pockets of her coverall.

I licked the blood off my fingertips. They were only oozing now, though very painful. I wondered how I would manage the climb down.

"Are you all right, Lisse?" Scylla examined my hand. "We need old Rich in the group to look after wounds like this."

"Even if Rich were here, he wouldn't be able to do anything. We should have a first-aid kit, I suppose." I licked my fingers again. "It's all right anyway."

"Just look at this view!" Katie interrupted, and we turned.

It was spectacular, with nothing between us and the far horizon in any direction. I felt we were getting the same view that the birds must have — the eagle's view.

During the time it had taken us to climb the mesa, the sun had moved from almost directly overhead into the southwest. Scylla found a sharp stone and, on a patch of dirt too thin for even the coarse mountain grass to grow, she scratched a long-tailed cross and marked the points of the compass on it.

"All right, everyone, what do you see?"

"A shining lake, due south."

"How far away?"

"Hard to say. Maybe six miles. Maybe more. This air is so clear, it's hard to judge."

"I can see a hollow, shadowed, a kind of ellipse. It's a

bit west of the lake and about the same distance away."

"All right. What else?"

"Due north it's all misty. That must mean more moisture. Maybe vegetation. But too far away to tell."

"There's a faint greenish color over there, to the northwest." I pointed. "A long way off. I couldn't even guess how far."

"Is that it?"

We all agreed that it was.

"Hmm. No rivers. Not even a stream. Nothing to eat either. We can manage without food for a while, but in this heat we really need water."

"There's the lake."

"Yes, that had better be our first objective. Although we've got nothing to store water in."

"Next time we come we'll be better prepared. Ropes. Waterbags. A first-aid kit."

"Let's get moving, then! We've got to get down off this thing first, and then there's a six-mile walk. Paul, before we leave, have you memorized the map?"

"Got it."

Paul's photographic memory was definitely going to give us an edge in The Game, I thought. If I don't cancel it with my clumsiness.

Going down was far more difficult than climbing up. We couldn't look up and plan our next move, but had to count on feeling with our feet, hoping that the toehold we picked was the right one. The sun was low in the west before Paul, who led the way this time, reached the bottom.

My right hand was throbbing. Hanging on was incredibly painful, and yet my fingertips, because of the damage to the nerve endings, were no longer sensitive to the delicate choice of whether a ledge was firm or flaking, whether or not it would be deep enough to support my hanging weight. Even in the cool shadow through which we climbed, I could feel the sweat running down my face and breasts.

I'd almost reached the bottom when my fingers finally let me down and I swung outward. I had time to scream a warning, so that those below me could get out of the way, and to think: I'm going to land on my back on the rocks and my spine will be broken. What a stupid waste!

There was no pain. Only a whirling sensation and blackness.

FOUR

July 2154. The Treasure Seekers

No *pain*. That was my first thought as I regained consciousness. *No pain means there's spinal cord damage. I'm a cripple for life and that's far, far worse than being unemployed.* I lay unmoving for what seemed like a long time. Then I forced a message through to my toes. *Wiggle*, I told them. They wiggled. *Kick!* My leg jerked. I curled my fingers and felt not sand but fabric.

"What happened?" I sat up and found I was sitting on the gray couch, staring at my friends. We were back at Barton Oaks.

"Lisse, are you all right?"

"Fine." I stared at the fingertips of my right hand. The skin was smooth and unscarred. It had all been a dream. If it had been real, I'd have been dead. I laughed uncertainly. "A desert. And a mesa. We climbed it. And I fell."

"That was my dream too."

"And mine. It's as clear—"

We were interrupted by the opening door. "Please come with me," the receptionist said in the flat, uninflected voice that robots everywhere seemed to have. Even though it was only a robot, we no longer felt able to talk freely in front of it. We followed it in silence down the softly lit hall and back to the changing rooms.

"You know what I think?" Katie said, as she unlaced her heavy boots and wriggled out of her coveralls.

"Don't tell us now. Wait till we're back home. If we discuss nothing until we're all together we'll get a clearer picture of what really happened," Karen advised.

"Darn!"

"What is it, Katie?"

"Remember that specimen of shrub I picked off the mesa? I could have sworn I put it in the top right-hand pocket of my coveralls."

"It's not there?"

"Not anywhere."

"Perhaps it fell out."

"It was buttoned down, Scylla."

"Do you suppose — ?"

"No discussion, Katie, remember. Not till we get home."

We met the boys in the hall and the door slid open for us. It was evident we were to leave. Brad hesitated. "We don't know when to come back."

We looked around. The robot had vanished. All the doors were closed. The changing lights glowed softly on the gray walls. The flowers wafted their sweetness through the warm air. The door stood insistently open.

"They'll get in touch with us. They did before."

As we waited for the train, I found I was staring at the clock. "Four o'clock."

"And we got here a bit before two-thirty, didn't we?" Brad picked up my thought. "Even allowing for the time it took to change out of our clothes and back again, and the Game Manager's talk, there's still *some* real time unaccounted for, isn't there?"

"Nowhere near the amount of time it felt like, Brad."

"But enough for a sleep and a dream."

"Wait till we get home," Scylla said again, and we boarded our train in silence. It was a slow one this time, stopping at a number of stations before reaching our DA. It was soon crowded with workers in dark suits or uniforms of one kind or another, carrying cases, bags, newspapers, and magazines. A middle-aged man sat down directly opposite us, stared, and shook open his newspaper as an obvious shield against the offending sight of eight unemployeds on *his* train.

We hadn't seen newspapers except for the tattered remains that blew about street corners, since we were only permitted to shop in Government stores, which didn't sell papers. The page-one headline screamed at me:

CONGRESSMAN CALLS FOR STERILIZATION OF THE UNEMPLOYED

Underneath, the feature article began, "Problem of overcrowding becomes critical . . ."

I felt myself turn cold. They're writing about *us*. They're trying to legislate *our* future and we don't have a say in it. We don't even have a *vote*.

I had often envied workers in the past, wondering what it must be like to live in your very own house, however small and dingy, to be able to watch television and read new books, to be allowed to go on vacation to different places, like the seaside.

Back in the old days, Karen had told us, people were free to travel wherever they wanted, as long as they had enough money to pay for it, and many of them did. Now only the workers had that privilege. It wasn't fair. They had everything and we had almost nothing. Yet it was evident from the article, as well as from the expressions on the faces of those sitting around us, that they despised us, maybe even hated us.

If we didn't exist, their tax money wouldn't have to pay for our basic shelter and food, I realized. Sterilization might be only the beginning. Perhaps, if they got their way, the workers would eliminate us entirely, like the Jews and Catholics and Gypsies who went to the gas chambers in the dark ages of the twentieth century.

I shrank into my corner, my eyes down, my hands clenched together, almost afraid to breathe, and, when the train stopped at our station, I jumped out ahead of the others and ran up the stairs, not stopping until I was on the street again.

"Hold on, Lisse. What's up?" Brad caught up with me and put his arm on my shoulder.

"Did you see that headline? Did you? They'll kill us all, that's what they'll do. . . ." It all poured out of me. I was shaking and couldn't stop.

"If only we could get together with other groups. There are enough of us."

"That's why we're isolated, Trent. It's no good. We've gone into this before."

"Aren't you even going to try? Are you going to sit back and be a victim, Paul? And the rest of you—are you just victims too?"

"Oh, stop it, you two." Scylla's voice was disgusted. "Do you want the thought police on you? Let's get home. We can talk about it there. *And* The Game."

Each of us wrote an account of our experience and, over a supper of beans and dumplings, we compared what we remembered. Allowing for minor memory lapses, our accounts tallied exactly.

"Which certainly takes care of the possibility of it being a dream."

"I thought we were being hypnotized at first, but . . ."

"The atmosphere was certainly right, Lisse. Soft colors, silence, pleasant scents."

"But why can I *still* feel the grittiness of the sand, the heat of the sun?"

And the pain, I thought, looking at my unscarred fingers. I can remember the pain. My eye caught Scylla's exotic mural of the courtyard with its orange trees in tubs. Now, in comparison with my memory of that *other* place, it looked garish and commonplace.

"Does it really matter if it's dream or hypnosis or something else?" I was almost crying. "It's real to *me*. I want to go back. I want to see the shining lake and find out what is beyond that mistiness to the north. I feel as if . . . as if it were *home*."

"Maybe we *shouldn't* question it too much. Perhaps The Game is like a soap bubble. If you poke it to see what the rainbows are made of, it bursts and you have nothing." Scylla understood what I felt.

The others argued, but since no one could add anything to our guesses, we went on to talk of the possibilities of The Game. The prize. The treasure. Our dearest wish . . .

"Like the pot of gold at the end of the rainbow," Paul said.

A pot of gold. Would that be as good as having a job? Paul seemed to think so. An endless supply of credits that would buy anything, even information and travel.

I went to bed imagining myself free to travel anywhere in the world, to see all the exotic places I had read about in the worm-riddled library books. To be able to spin the globe and stop it with a finger and say, "There. I choose to leave here and go *there*."

Did the desert and the mesa and the silver-edged lake exist somewhere in Africa or China? Was the place we had visited a copy of somewhere in the real world? Or just an imaginary place culled from the needs and dreams of our group? A never-never land? All I knew was that it called me. And, in spite of their scientific arguments and objections, I knew it called the others.

I dreamed that night of hot sun and spicy herbs and woke to the smell of paint. Scylla had painted out her mural and was beginning to transpose to the end wall of the warehouse *her* vision of our newfound country.

"Oh, yes, Scylla. Yes, that is it exactly!" As I watched it grow beneath her paintbrush I forgot to eat.

Paul was also up early and had pinned a large sheet of paper to one of the work tables. I put away my breakfast dishes and watched what he was doing. He had drawn a compass rose in the upper right corner and, using a ruler to measure distances, he was marking the features we had observed from the top of the mesa. He was whistling softly and looked happier than I'd seen him since we'd left school.

On the other hand, Katie was totally frustrated. "Without any real samples, I'm just guessing," she moaned.

"Why?" I asked.

"Oh, Lisse, isn't it obvious that without samples—"

"No, I mean, *why* did they remove the samples from your pockets?"

"They didn't really though, did they?" Trent interrupted. "If it was all in our heads, we couldn't get real samples, could we?"

"It's so muddled. I *know* I was there. My fingers still feel it."

"We're talking in circles again," Brad interrupted. "What we should do is plan a strategy. Think it out ahead of time so that we're ready for the clues when we see them. After all, we don't know how long we'll be there next time. Or how many chances we get."

"And the first thing we should do is get in better shape," Alden said. "I'm sure I wasn't the only one totally pooped at the top of that mesa."

So we jogged through the dingy streets of our DA. After a week we were doing three miles. After a month we'd got it up to six. Brad and Trent scrounged some rope, tackle, and weights and set up a gym at the other end of the warehouse.

We were busy, healthier than we'd ever been, and although Paul and Trent still argued with Brad and Alden, they were now creative arguments, not the mindless snarling that had gone on before our first visit to Barton Oaks.

But nothing happened. One morning, with a cold drizzle outside, Trent pulled the blankets over his head and refused to get up. "It's stupid. Why kill myself for nothing?"

"We're bound to get another invitation soon." I couldn't bear the thought of *not* going back to that magic country of sand and sun and I screamed at Trent, tearing the blanket off him.

"Suppose we don't?" Katie asked bluntly. "Suppose that was it?"

"Oh, Katie, I think I'll *die*."

"Why would they stop?"

"Did we do something wrong?"

"How can we tell? We don't know the rules. It's hopeless."

"No way!" Brad opened the door. "Come on. Out we

go. See if we can make eight miles today."

We were over the hump and by the time the second invitation finally came, mysteriously slipped through the grille of the elevator door, we were strong, capable, and confident that we could cope with any challenge The Game might bring.

We had already decided that, if we were given a choice, we would head directly for the shining lake. Brad argued that, if we were to stay any time at all, water was the greatest priority. Karen disagreed, saying that although we might *feel* we'd been without water for days, it was obviously no more than an hour. We still could not agree on that basic point: had our adventure been real?

We compromised by taking water bottles as well as pencil and paper, protein bars, and a first-aid kit. A good theory, but it didn't work. We arrived at Barton Oaks, changed out of our street clothes, and stored the stuff we had brought with us in the pockets of our coveralls. Feeling smug and ready for anything, we lay back on our reclining chairs, closed our eyes, and instantly, it seemed, felt the hot sun on our faces and the sand beneath our backs.

We sat up and looked eagerly around. This time the mesa was some six miles north of us, etched clearly against the misty background. To left and right, the brown sand met the brilliant sky in a line that quivered with heat.

We turned. There, no more than ten minutes' walk away, was the shining lake. "Almost as if they knew our plans."

"Which is crazy."

"Yes. But how else . . . ?"

It was an extraordinary place. The surface of the water was very still, reflecting the sky in blinding blue-white, like a sheet of molten metal. What we had thought was a froth of wavelets along the shore had no movement. Like frozen foam. It wasn't until we got close that we could see the waves were really a thick deposit of salty crystals. From a distance they reflected the sun as dazzling white, although as we got closer we could see that the white was streaked with garish shades of yellow, orange, and green.

"Let's swim," I suggested. "I've always wanted to swim in a real lake, haven't you?"

"Great idea!" Scylla began to unlace her boots.

"No, don't!" Alden's voice was sharp. "It's salt. Like the Dead Sea. So full of minerals that nothing can live in it."

"People swim in the sea, don't they? That's salty."

"Not like this. This is a chemical soup. It'll itch and burn. And we don't have enough fresh water to wash it off."

It was so tantalizing. I bent down, not quite believing Alden, touched the water and licked my fingers. My tongue burned and my mouth watered. I spat and spat. The obnoxious taste reminded me of the salts they used to give us at school for upset stomachs. I reached into the knee pocket that held my water flask.

"My water bottle's gone."

"So's mine."

We checked. None of the supplies we had so carefully

tucked into our coveralls had come through to the Game world.

"So we can't bring anything in. And we can't take anything out."

"Which proves it's a dream," said Karen triumphantly.

"Or hypnosis."

"Either way, what's the point?" Trent was almost smug. "I told you guys we were wasting our time, but you wouldn't listen." He sat down on the sand.

"You can't stay there."

"Sure I can. When the rest of you have finished stumbling about in the heat, I'll be here."

"I agree with Trent. It's terribly unscientific." Alden was cross, faced with an unknown chemical soup that he couldn't do a thing with.

"No!" Scylla was firm. "Whatever this place is, there are clues to be looked for, a treasure to be found. Come on, you two. We don't know how long we've got."

With no more than an occasional grumble, we set off at a brisk pace toward our next goal, the shadowy ellipse to the northwest. As we plodded through the hot sand I told myself that, objectively, less than half an hour had passed, that in fact I was lying on a soft couch in a cool room at Barton Oaks. My body disagreed. I licked my dry lips and wondered what would happen if we *did* die of thirst. We'd have lost The Game. That was certain. I began to giggle foolishly.

"What's so funny, Lisse?"

"I don't know what you get for winning at The Game. But I know what the booby prize is. You're dead!"

"If they play for keeps." Brad took my joke seriously. "But they brought us back last time rather than have you injured. If you *can* be injured in a dream. If this *is* a dream."

"I'm sure they won't let us die out here," Paul gasped. "It'd be so . . . so messy and unfinished."

"I hope you're right."

We trudged on. The sand became firmer and easier to walk on. We crossed occasional ridges of stones, which got closer to each other as we approached the dark area. Then, suddenly, we were upon it, standing on a knife edge between light and dark. Behind us was sun-baked sand, ridged with countless stones, gray and reddish-brown. At our feet an abrupt cliff led down to a perfectly circular pit. It was as if a giant had used a huge spoon and scooped a serving of sand a half mile or more across out of the desert floor.

I picked up a rock and threw it. It bounced once and then fell, down, down. It was a long time before it stopped. Red dust powdered my fingers. "Look."

"That's iron," Katie exclaimed. "Look, here's another piece. And another. It must have been an enormous iron meteorite. I wonder if it all broke up or if there's a core of iron down there at the bottom?"

"Want to go down and look, Katie? It's not as steep as the mesa."

"And there might be water at the bottom."

"I doubt it. We'd see greenery. No, if we want water we're going to have to walk north to get it. As far as the misty country."

"How many miles is that, do you suppose?"

"More than we can walk without water. I don't care if this *is* a dream. I'm dying of—" Brad's voice was suddenly cut off.

Thirst. I finished his sentence for him in my mind and realized that it was no longer true. My lips and tongue were no longer swollen. I wasn't even particularly thirsty. I opened my eyes and saw that we were back at Barton Oaks.

Back home, we argued again about the reality of our experience. "I've never even *dreamed* of thirst like that," Alden argued.

"And how can we experience places like the salt lake and the meteor crater, with all the details right?" I appealed to Katie, the geologist, and Alden, the chemist. "In a dream, events are random, fantastical. This *is* real. Somehow we're being taken to a real place."

"How?"

"I don't know. But it is real and no one's going to change my mind about that."

"If only we had samples. . . ."

"It's obvious they don't want us to bring anything back. There has to be a reason for that."

"Perhaps that's why we have to change our clothes. So we can't bring back dust on our sandals, a twig or a leaf maybe."

"Next time let's ask the manager to let us take water-bags and a first-aid kit. See what kind of reaction we get."

While we waited for the next summons, Paul extended his map and Scylla made drawings as exact as any photograph could have been. Katie and Alden read what they could find on meteors and Dead Sea ecology.

This time there were no arguments. Whatever The Game was, it had sucked us in. We were totally committed to it. We breathed, we talked The Game. And, of course, we exercised. Now we could jog twelve miles and climb the brick wall at the end of the warehouse. Our appetites were enormous, far beyond the reality of our food credits, and we sold more of Scylla's paintings and Brad's carved wooden toys and puzzles to workers leaving the subway so that we could buy extra food.

We had left school plump, pale, and more or less unmotivated. Now we were lean and keen. The Game had become our life. Everything we did sprang from some need of The Game. Sometimes I wondered what would happen to us if we never got another invitation. If, somehow, without knowing it, we had failed a test. A week went by. And another. Again Trent and Paul began bickering. Scylla lost her temper for the first time since I'd known her and told them to go out and sell Brad's toys and not come back until they were in a better mood.

At last the summons came. As soon as we arrived at Barton Oaks we asked to see the Game Manager and explained our needs. "With waterbags we could stay longer and learn more."

"And we should have a first-aid kit. If there were a serious accident—"

"You have a trained medic? You can improvise, surely."

We looked blankly at each other. Governments know

everything. They don't make mistakes.

The Manager looked at his file. "There *used* to be a medic in your group. But his father put in a priority claim on his services."

Our laughter interrupted him. "Oh, Rich! Imagine old Rich climbing that mesa!"

"As to your request," the Manager went on, "I'm afraid I must deny it. You're not the first to ask, you know. But to allow outside materials into The Game would upset the balance, skew the success-probability . . ." He murmured a stream of mathematical gobbledygook. What he meant was NO. A flat and categorical NO. No cameras, no water, no paper, not even a first-aid kit. And we could bring back only what we could carry in our minds. That was that. The Game on his terms was better than no Game at all. We didn't argue. Meekly we stripped off our clothes, dressed in coveralls and boots, and lay down on our reclining chairs.

This time we opened our eyes to a river valley that had been dry for so long that nothing grew in it but a few silvery thorn bushes. Only the water-rounded boulders told us that this must once have been a great river.

"And the salt lake was once part of the sea. The land between must have hunched up and cut off the lake and the river," Katie told us.

We walked between the boulders toward the misty lands to the north. Slowly the ground became less arid. Short, spiky grasses, with edges so barbed they cut your fingers if you tried to pluck them, replaced cactus and thorn.

We walked steadily, in a rhythm that we could keep up for hours if we needed to. The air was clean and spicy, and we strode along, arms swinging, breathing deeply, not talking very much, just enjoying the sense of space and incredible, unaccustomed freedom. Until Paul stumbled and sprawled headlong.

"Are you all right? What happened?"

"I tripped over something. Something heavy and hard, too. I can feel it through my boot." He hopped on one foot.

We knelt and scuffed back grass and sand. Just beneath the surface was an extraordinary, bubbly mass of metal, greenish above the surface, pinky-gold beneath. Together we tugged at it and finally pulled it free.

"Copper!" exclaimed Katie, after spitting on the lump and rubbing it clean. "Native copper!"

"Then there *are* people here? Do you suppose they're friendly?" I looked anxiously around. The grass that fringed the dry riverbed was at least a yard high. It would be possible for a person to hide in it and creep closer and closer. . . .

Katie laughed. "Native copper just means copper occurring naturally on the surface, not having to be mined and smelted. If there are many big lumps around, it's really a sign that the country's uninhabited. Copper's so valuable, so easy to shape, that it would have all been picked up and used by now if there were people here."

I stopped looking over my shoulder every few minutes. I'd read so many adventures about Africa—and this place *felt* like Africa—that I was expecting anything to happen.

Nothing did. We left the riverbed and walked through knee-high grass, heavy and ripe. Katie picked some stalks and rubbed the tips between the palms of her hands until the husks fell away. She blew them off her hand and ate the creamy kernels that remained.

"Oh, do be careful!"

"Don't worry. I've never heard of a poisonous grass. It's delicious, in fact. I wish I knew more about farming, whether this grain could actually be useful, like wheat or barley or oats."

"Benta would have known." Saying her name out loud reminded me how much I still missed Benta. The others were all so much cleverer that it was sometimes a struggle to keep up, like dog-paddling in the swimming pool at school while the others did the crawl. With Benta I had been able to relax and be myself.

"I wish she were here, Katie."

"So do I, Lisse. I miss her too. And, as you say, she'd have known."

We walked on, rubbing handfuls of grain between our palms and munching on the ripe kernels. We were getting close to what we had called the misty lands. The mist itself was no longer visible as a band across the horizon, but the air was cooler and fresher and the sky a softer blue, the harsh sun haloed with gold.

Now we walked on soft turf, interspersed with strange tall grasses and an occasional tree. Dew soaked our boots and coveralls. Birds were singing in the bushes. Insects buzzed in the grass but didn't bother us or bite.

"I wonder if there are flowers. If so, there should be fruit, and some of it might be edible."

"Here's some, Katie. On this bush." As Paul stretched out his hand, a flock of tiny birds, not much larger than bees, rose in a cloud and settled on a bush farther ahead. "And if the birds are eating them, they must be safe to—"

"Don't!" Katie screamed, but Paul already had a handful in his mouth.

Her scream cut through the misty sky and the golden sun, through the spicy scents and the dew-laden grass. We were back in the twilight gray of the Game room.

"Drat it," Katie said crossly. "I wish you'd remembered what I said about not eating berries, Paul."

"But the birds—"

"It's probably safe to eat what primates eat. But certainly not birds. They can excrete poisons like prussic acid that'll kill a person outright."

"You don't know that those particular berries—" began Paul argumentatively.

"Oh, yes, we do. We only come back here when someone's in danger. You of all people should have remembered that."

"Enough," Scylla interrupted pacifically. "It was a great experience. Don't spoil it. Let's get home. We've got so much to remember and discuss."

FIVE

July 2154.
The Archbishop or the Grasshopper?

It was raining when we came out of the subway, a fine, ruthless rain that felt like nothing at first but within five minutes had soaked and chilled us to the bone. It seemed to intensify the city smell, made up of garbage, crowded humanity, and old buildings slowly decaying. Never had the gray houses, stores, and factories looked so ugly and hopeless. I could have sat down in a doorway and wept for the loss of the sun, the blue sky, the clean air, and the limitless horizon we had left behind in Barton Oaks.

We trudged silently along, water dripping off the ends of our hair and trickling down our necks, so we didn't see him until we were almost on top of him. A dark shape huddled against the steel door of the warehouse, *our* warehouse.

Brad advanced cautiously and touched the figure with his toe, while the rest of us stood alert, ready to fight if we had to. It didn't seem likely that Charlie would have sent one of his thugs to camp on our doorstep, but you never knew. The figure groaned, unfolded itself, staggered to its feet, and stared at us through the drizzle.

"It *is* you! Where the heck have you been all afternoon?" It was the unmistakable voice of Rich, the would-be psychiatrist.

Perhaps if we had been less wet and less miserable we might have made a better show of welcoming him, regardless of our feelings. As it was, I managed a feeble "Hi, Rich," and Scylla said, "What on earth are *you* doing here, slumming?" in her deepest and most dramatic tones, while the other six stood with their mouths open.

"Aren't you going to ask me in?" Rich's laugh was forced.

"Sorry. You surprised us, that's all. Welcome to our castle." Brad unlocked the outer door and we crowded in out of the mizzling rain.

If Rich was impressed by the security, or by our furnishings and general coziness, he didn't let on. He strolled around the big room, leaving puddles on the floor, while the rest of us got out of our sopping clothes and hung everything in front of the electric stove, whose burners Scylla had switched on as soon as we got home.

Wrapped in blankets, we sat and toweled our hair and stared at Rich. He stood in the middle of the floor, his hands in his pants pockets, stretching the fabric so that it outlined his pudgy bottom. It was a self-conscious pose that had always irritated me at school, but, looking at him now, I realized that it was just an act, that underneath he was scared to death.

"So where's the limo?" Trent inquired. "Your driver gone for a drink?"

"Actually, I've . . ." Rich's shoulders sagged. He looked around uncertainly. "I've come to stay. That is, if you'll have me," he added quickly.

"How did you know where we lived?" Karen's question filled the stunned silence.

"I got a notice. Telling me to report to this address. I didn't know it was a *warehouse*. Didn't know it was *you* till I heard your voices. Do you really *live* here?"

"Of course we do. But why were you told to report here? Are you supposed to psychoanalyze us?"

Rich's face got red. He turned his back on us and stared at Scylla's mural. If it had been anyone but Rich I'd have hugged him and said it was all right, whatever the trouble was.

"Actually, I'm not going to be a psychiatrist. They've given my father a robot assistant. I've been turned out. Got a notice yesterday, with a ticket and this address. I had to leave everything behind. My clothes, my chess set. My holo-player. And when I got here no one answered the door. I waited for *hours*."

Trent exploded. "A robot psychiatrist? You've been replaced by . . . by a . . ." He doubled up.

Laughter is contagious at the best of times. Looking at old Rich, we just couldn't help ourselves.

"Imagine lying on a couch talking to a robot. . . ." gasped Alden.

"It'd work beautifully. You'd say 'Doctor, I feel bad.' Then the robot would say, in a *very* sympathetic voice, 'You feel bad?' By the time the session was over, with the

robot agreeing to everything you said, you'd feel a lot better, wouldn't you? That's how it works, doesn't it, Rich?"

Before Paul had finished talking, Rich was at the elevator door. I ran after him. "Where d'you think you're
going?"

"Out of this nuthouse. Anywhere. I don't care."

That set Trent and Paul and Alden off again.

"Oh, do shut up, you three," I interrupted. "Rich, you
can't leave now. It's getting dark. You can't go out alone.
And you've had nothing to eat, I bet. And where do you
plan to sleep?"

"I don't know. I don't care," he said again.

"At least stay for supper." I took his hand, which I'd
never have done under normal circumstances. It was
clammy and cold. I managed to coax him close to the
stove and told Brad to help him out of his wet clothes and
into a blanket.

Paul and I started chopping turnips and potatoes for
supper. We'd picked up a package of soytein with some of
the money we'd earned from Brad's toys, so with the veg-
etables there'd be a good stew tonight. Brad mopped the
puddles off the floor and hung Rich's clothes up to dry. As
for the rest, they sat around in a disorganized bunch. It
was different now that Rich was here, like a busy hive
into which an intruder bee had wandered.

Rich ate his stew in horrified silence, then went over to
feel his clothes. They were still soaking, of course.

"You can't go anyway, Rich. You *have* to stay. Don't
you see? You were given a ticket and *our* address. By the

Government. It must be because of The Game." Everyone looked blank until I explained. "We needed a medic, remember? And the Manager was mixed up. He thought Rich was already part of the group."

They got it then, all except Rich. We tried to explain The Game to him, all talking at once, trying to explain to him just how *real* it was. And how important in our lives.

"Sounds to me as if the lot of you've been brainwashed. I've never heard such nonsense in my life. Maybe you *do* need a psychiatrist, but it certainly isn't going to be me." He grabbed at his damp trousers.

While we were arguing with Rich, Scylla was sitting by the stove, combing out her damp hair. After the rain it stood out around her head like a fiery halo. Her sudden exclamation interrupted us.

"Oh, that hurt! There's something in my hair. What on earth is it?"

It was a patch of gummy stuff, greenish against the copper of her hair. It stuck to my fingers when I tried to get it out, and Scylla winced.

"Perhaps it's something from the Game world," I suggested. "Like tree gum. That'd prove it was real, Rich."

"Lisse, you're a romantic idiot. You always were." Rich looked at Scylla's temple. "So are you all. You and your 'Game.' D'you know what this stuff really is? It's electrolytic jelly, that's what. I've used it myself, dozens of times. It's to make a good contact between diagnostic electrodes and human skin." He looked around at our stunned expressions and smiled. "Oh, you can get it off with a little alcohol, by the way."

We stared, not quite understanding, perhaps not wanting to understand.

"What fools you are!" He gestured toward Scylla's new mural of the view from the mesa and to the map on which Paul had been working. "Look at all the time you've been wasting! On what? On a computer-induced dream experience, that's all. You haven't really *been* anywhere. You haven't really *seen* anything. You've been lying on couches with electrodes attached to your stupid skulls."

"I don't believe you. It's real. It *has* to be. If it isn't real what have we got?" I suddenly saw our factory home through Rich's eyes, dingy, makeshift, second-rate. "The Game country's real, Rich, more real than this."

Paul had followed my line of thought. "The archbishop is asleep and dreaming of a grasshopper that is sitting on his chest," he said. "Or is he? Perhaps it is the grasshopper who dreams that it is sitting on the chest of a sleeping archbishop. Which of them is real? The archbishop? Or the grasshopper?"

Rich laughed. "Typical response, Paul. When in doubt think abstract. As typical as Scylla's art. All of you . . . you're so utterly predictable. And *you* brought me here? If it's true, which I doubt, believe me, I'll be talking to the authorities in the morning. I'll be gone so fast. . . ."

Brad's fists doubled over, Scylla's eyes flashed, and Paul and Trent opened their mouths to start one of their interminable arguments. *Oh, no!*

Karen laughed. "Don't let him get to you. As for you, Rich, you'd better save your breath and get some sleep.

We can only offer you a sofa for tonight. Tomorrow, well, you can talk to the authorities all you want, but I bet you're here to stay. We'll teach you the art of scrounging and hope we can come up with an extra mattress. After our run, that is. You see, we jog twelve miles every other day and work out in our gym the alternate days."

Clever Karen. At the thought of pudgy Rich following our daily routine we all relaxed and smiled, said goodnight, and trailed off to bed, leaving Rich to curl up on the sagging sofa.

I lay awake, wondering. Did the gum in Scylla's hair prove that the Game world wasn't real? But if it wasn't, then why had the Government sent for Rich? Why was he important to the group? I listened to the shrieks and songs of city nightlife until dawn.

In the morning, Rich grunted and moaned and pulled the blanket over his head to hide the light that filtered through the warehouse's dirty windows. We left him and set out on our own.

"What Rich said about computer dreaming," Brad panted as we took the first three blocks at a trot, "I don't think it matters, even if it is true."

"I wish it wasn't. But it does make sense of everything peculiar, like my fingers being healed and not being able to take things to the other place or bring them back. . . ."

"It's still an adventure. It's not something out of our minds. More like reading an exciting story, wondering how it'll turn out."

"But why've they done it? Why such an elaborate

scheme just to entertain us? I think there's more to The Game than meets the eye. Even if we know *how* it's done, we still don't know *why*." Karen sounded emphatic. "The more I think about it, the less sense the Manager's explanation about war games and so on makes."

When we got back, Rich had already been to the Government Center. His face was grim. "They say I have to stay here. But I don't have to be part of your nonsense, and I won't. It's your fault, you idiots. You've ruined my life."

If he hadn't sounded so melodramatic we might have felt sorrier for him. "You'd have been better off running with us," Brad said as he toweled down.

"You must be joking."

"You'll be sorry when you have to cross six miles of desert or climb a cliff," Trent warned him.

"In your precious 'Game,' you mean?" Rich laughed. "You still haven't got it, have you? You don't *use* your muscles. You're prone on a couch. Something I intend to practice a lot." He stretched himself out luxuriously.

"But we *are* in better shape during The Game than we were to begin with. Maybe it just means that they feed our physical condition into the machinery or whatever makes it happen."

"Oh, don't waste your breath on Rich. He'll find out soon enough. Right now it's your turn to sweep, Trent. Here." Katie handed him the broom. "When we've cleaned up and eaten we'll take you out scrounging, Rich. Unless you fancy spending the rest of your life on that sofa. And we've got to get you some new clothes."

"What's wrong with these? This is a top-quality suit, ten percent *real* wool."

"It doesn't matter if it's ten percent feathers, you can't wear it outside. It's against the law to wear working clothes when you're not a worker. You've got to get your identity card for this DA. And food credit cards. It's going to be a busy day, so you'd better get moving."

At Scylla's briskness, Rich's pompous act collapsed like a leaky balloon. "They already gave me a card and credits," he muttered.

It rained all week and Rich wouldn't budge. It was an uncomfortable time, like living on a scale that wouldn't balance. Us on one side and Rich on the other. Sometimes he'd be up, lecturing on at us about what he called "the real world," until I felt like leaving him at the Purple Orange or the Coffee Bush and letting him find out for himself what "reality" was. Then sometimes he'd be down, bewildered and morose, and I'd feel guilty, even though I still wanted to shake him.

On the sixth day we found the now familiar envelope on the floor of the elevator when we got back from jogging. "And one for you, Rich." Alden handed out the familiar invitations and travel tokens.

"You're joking! Do you really think I'm going to submit to having *my* brains fried and filled with spurious messages about nonexistent places?"

"It's not like that, Rich. . . ." I stopped, with no words to describe the magic of the clean air, the space, of a country not yet used up and spoiled by human beings.

"Hey, there's one extra!" Alden exclaimed.

"One what?"

"Invitation. Why, it's addressed to Benta!"

"Let me see." I snatched the envelope from Alden. "But she's not *here*. She's farming somewhere in the Midwest. Could they have made a mistake?"

"Why so surprised, Lisse? They make mistakes all the time. Like replacing me with a moronic robot. Anyway, why are you all so sure that it *is* the Government? Did you hear about The Game through official channels?"

We looked at each other. "N-no. Not exactly."

"There you are then. The people running this Game thing may be some black-market outfit with nothing whatever to do with the Government."

"But why would they do it?" Karen asked in the silence.

"Money. Power. What other motives are there?"

I sighed. It was hard to like Rich, no matter how I tried. "But The Game costs us nothing," I protested.

"And nobody but the Government could organize transport or set up a place like Barton Oaks," Brad put in. "It's rich, in a quiet way. You're wrong, Rich, it *has* to be the Government."

We were still arguing as we set out in feeble sunshine to scrounge for a mattress and bedding. Seeing our Designated Area in daylight shook Rich. He seemed to shrink noticeably as we walked past grimy warehouses and stores with broken windows. We found a food store that would sell us a package of protein powder, and the rest of us cheered. Potatoes and turnips are filling, but a body needs protein, too.

Rich was aghast. "What about meat? Just a small steak? A tiny leg of spring lamb?"

I felt sorry for him until, an hour later, he turned down the third mattress we'd found for him. This one was brand new, only waterstained in one corner, so that the pattern of the cover had run. It was obviously a worker's top-grade mattress, better than any of the ones we'd found before.

"All right," said Brad. "We'll take it home anyway. If you don't want it, one of us will have it and you can have the extra. If you're too fussy for *that,* you can sleep on the floor. Now grab the back end and heave."

By the time we'd gone two blocks, Rich's knees were sagging and he was puffing so hard I thought he'd have a heart attack, so Scylla and I took turns holding the rear end while Alden took the front.

Home was just around the corner when we heard the clatter of helicopter blades overhead. *The thought police.* Instinctively we crouched in the shadow of a warehouse wall. My skin prickled and I wondered why I felt guilty? Surely we'd done nothing wrong? We were in our own DA and the mattress we were carrying had been honestly scrounged. But I had that rat-in-a-maze feeling again. All I wanted to do was to find a hole and hide in it.

"It's all right, Lisse." Scylla's voice was steady and I took a deep breath.

Dust fanned up by the helicopter blades swirled around our feet. Dust and stray pieces of paper. DOWN WITH THE GOVERNMENT. WORK FOR THE UNEMPLOYED. They were printed in the blotched letters of some underground protest group's homemade press. We trampled them into the dirt and turned the corner.

The helicopter had come down directly in front of *our* warehouse. We stopped. Was it a raid? Had we done something wrong without knowing it? Something bad enough to warrant a raid? But it was all right. The helicopter rose straight into the air to the level of the second-story windows, then veered out of sight beyond the roofs.

"There's someone . . . Scylla, it's Benta!"

I dropped my end of the mattress without a thought and ran forward. How healthy she looked, her cheeks rosy and weather-beaten. The freckles, which had stood out like crayon marks on her white face the last time I had seen her, had faded into the all-over tan of her face. I put my arms around her.

"Oh, Benta!"

"Watch out," she said tremulously. "My basket. The eggs . . . if they're not cracked already . . ." Her eyes brimmed with tears.

"It's all right. Forget the stupid eggs. There's nothing to cry about. You're *here*."

She bit her lip and tried to smile. "Sorry."

"Come in. Oh, I'm so happy to see you. What are you doing here? Did the police bring you? There isn't anything wrong, is there?" I shepherded her into the elevator and upstairs, took her basket and cloak from her, and sat her down close to the stove, which I switched on. It was quite warm outside today, but she was shivering.

"Did they actually give you permission to visit us? That's amazing!" My voice died as she shook her head.

"The've robotized the farm. Just walked in this week without notice. Instead of mixed farming we're to grow turnips—what a waste! They're letting Dad stay on as manager, but they turned me out. Of my own home, Lisse. They gave me a ticket and an address and told me to leave. Oh, Lisse, isn't the city awful! It was dark when the bus dropped me off, and there were horrible, crazy people everywhere. I got lost. So then I knocked on a door and this old lady let me in. I guess I was lucky she trusted me. I left as soon as it was light. I felt safer then. Only a few workers around. Then this gang suddenly . . . their faces were painted. I dropped the basket and tried to run. That's when I think the eggs got broken . . ."

"It doesn't *matter*, Benta. We'll make an omelette. An enormous omelette." I hugged her, but she drew back.

"Then the helicopter arrived and they ran away. So the men picked me up and took me to a huge building and asked me all sorts of questions. Then they brought me here."

"I'm so sorry you lost your job, Benta, but you know you have a home with us. It's not bad, really it isn't. Much better than I'd expected. Usually it *is* safe during the day, and Katie has taught us karate, so we know how to look out for ourselves in a pinch."

Then Scylla swept over and exclaimed at the basket of

food that Benta had brought. "Butter. And a jar of *real* cream. A dozen eggs. A whole dozen! And cheese. I'll make fresh noodles. We have a little flour that's not too stale. Alden, you must help me with the sauce. We'll use the cracked eggs and the cream and some of the butter. They won't keep. A special dinner to celebrate your joining us, Benta. And you too, Rich," she added politely.

After weeks of turnip stew, however cleverly disguised, the pasta with cream sauce was wonderful. I had forgotten just how full and satisfied cream and butter can make you feel. Back in school we had them on very special holidays, a memorable break from the dreary institutional cooking of the rest of the year.

At bedtime we unanimously voted that Benta should have the new mattress and that Rich, who had been so difficult about it, would have to spend another night on the sofa.

Tomorrow, I realized, as I snuggled down under my blanket, was the day to go to Barton Oaks. The ten of us. There was a roundness in the number ten that made me feel good. But something niggled at the corner of my mind. Something too slick to be merely coincidence. Only I couldn't pin it down.

I woke in the middle of the night. The thought police were out. I could hear the clatter of helicopter blades and see the occasional flare of light across the room as the helicopter's searchlight lit up the warren of streets below. It was a sight and sound so familiar that it normally never woke me anymore.

I sat up and realized that it was Benta, in the next bed,

who had wakened me. I reached over and touched her hand. It was icy cold. She was rigid and shivering.

"It's all right," I whispered. "We're safe here. As safe as in a medieval castle with a moat and drawbridge and . . ." What was it called? " . . . and a portcullis."

She slept after that. I could hear her breathing slow down, become regular. But now *I* couldn't sleep. I had suddenly remembered two unrelated incidents that had happened during The Game. The first one was after I had slipped and hurt my hand. Someone—who was it? I couldn't remember—had said that we should have a doctor along.

And Rich had arrived, his job made redundant by a robot.

The second incident was when we had discovered the grasses and Katie had said we really needed someone with a farming background. And here was Benta. Delivered safely to our door by the thought police.

I couldn't get it out of my head and told the others in the morning. It was stupid. I wasn't thinking.

Benta turned white and stared at me as if she despised me. "Dad's and my life spoiled for a stupid *game?*"

"The arrogance of it." Rich stormed. "My career ruined. Why did you have to remember *me?*"

"But what power!" Karen exclaimed. "The Game must be far more important than bread and circuses in order for the Government to move people from place to place as if they were pieces in a mysterious game of chess."

"What *can* it mean?" I asked.

"Does it matter?" Benta was in tears." Does it really matter, Lisse? You haven't seen your family since you went to school. But I have. I've been home. Dad loves me. He *needs* me. And now I'll never see him again. Oh, why did you have to think of me?"

SIX

Autumn and Winter 2154.
The Milk of Paradise

W e almost had to drag Benta and Rich with us on the now-familiar train to Barton Oaks. Benta was listless and numb and looked at me so coldly I could hardly bear it. I found myself echoing her accusation. Why did we have to think of her?

Rich was vociferous. "Over my dead body," he shouted. "Those power-hungry bureaucrats have manipulated my life. I'm not going to let them manipulate my *mind*."

We got them onto the train, mostly because they were startled by the subway system and subdued by the glares of traveling workers. "It's wonderful," I whispered to Benta, holding her cold hand. "It's like . . . all your dreams come true."

She drew her hand away and turned to stare into the darkness beyond the window. Rich heard and mocked in an undertone. "Dreams come true. Listen to yourself, Lisse. They've brainwashed you, turned your mind to soup, and you don't even know it!"

If it *is* brainwashing I won't give in, I thought savagely when we got to Barton Oaks and, when the gray couch unfolded backward until I was reclining, I swore I wouldn't let myself be hypnotized. I stared at the ceiling, concentrating on the patterns of light, counting the repetitions. I won't . . . I won't. Then I blinked and was staring up at soft blue sky.

It's not real, I told myself. It's an illusion, I said. I drew in a breath of damp spicy air that set my toes and fingers tingling. The desert and the grassland were behind us now, and we had awakened—or been transported—to the edge of the mysterious misty lands. Ahead of us rolled acres of parkland, set with trees whose branches spread wide above the short bluish-green turf.

Benta clutched me, and I could swear that her nails digging into the flesh of my arm were real. No dream. No hypnosis.

"Lisse, am I dreaming? It *is* so beautiful! And those are nut trees. Like the ones on the farm. Before they cut them down."

She ran across the grass, her arms wide, and embraced the trunk, running her fingers down its smooth bark. She laughed. "It *feels* real. Oh, Lisse, it *is* real, isn't it?"

I took a deep breath of sweet untainted air and nodded. "You bet it's real, Benta." I was persuading myself as well as her. I pushed the memory of the gum in Scylla's hair out of my mind. If the dingy streets, the factory, the craziness of nightlife in our DA were real and this was *not*, then life was meaningless. I laughed. "As real as real!"

Then I saw Rich. He sat hunched over, looking down, not at the vista ahead, his hands clasped together. "Rich, are you okay?" Karen bent over him and shook his shoulder. When he moved away from her hand, I saw that he was taking his pulse.

Poor Rich. "It's *not* hypnosis. It's *not* a dream." I yanked him to his feet. "Just look for yourself." *It must be real,* I wanted to shout. *Tell me it's real, Rich.*

Only when Benta cried out, "And there are ripe nuts on the ground!" and the others ran forward, did Rich lumber after them. I followed him to where the others were squatting on the grass. I picked up a fallen nut, peeled off the rind, and broke open the shell. The meat inside was crisp and sweet as Paradise.

Into my mind flashed a couplet from a nineteenth-century poem I had found in the library. How did it go? "Beware, beware . . . something, something . . . for he on honeydew has fed and drunk the milk of Paradise."

Paradise. I got uneasily to my feet and walked on. The great gray trunk of one tree sparkled in the sun. I put out an exploratory hand and touched a sticky lump. I broke it off and touched it with my tongue. *Honey.* I looked up and saw the combs, lodged in a crack between two branches, bees buzzing attentively around. It was too perfect, as if someone was reading my mind.

Go away, I snarled inwardly. *Leave us alone. Don't spoil this place. It's the only joy we've got.*

Then the others crowded around, picking at the hardened drops of honey on the tree trunk. Trent was all for climbing the tree and breaking off a comb, but the rest of us dissuaded him.

"You've got no protection. You could get stung."

"I'm not afraid of a sting or two."

"What about ten or twenty?" Rich warned. "You could go into anaphylactic shock and die, and I wouldn't be able to do a thing to help you." Then he realized what he was saying and stopped. "Go ahead. The bees aren't real. Their stings won't be either."

"In any case, when we've been in danger before we've just found ourselves back at Barton Oaks. It'd be stupid to let that happen before we've found any more clues," I added.

"What clues?" Rich naturally asked.

"The Game is like a treasure hunt. Every time we come here we look for clues that will help us find the treasure."

"Such as?"

"Well, first there was the mesa. It was like a map of the desert to tell us where to go next. Then there was the salt lake and the meteor crater . . ."

"And the grasslands . . ." Katie put in.

"That's not much of a clue."

"The dry riverbed where I fell over the native copper, remember?" said Alden.

"What about today?"

"Honey and nut trees, I suppose."

"I think it's *all* nuts," Rich retorted automatically, but I could tell that his mind was working.

We walked on slowly through patches of parkland and forest. It was too beautiful to hurry. I stopped thinking about being a rat in a maze and began to enjoy myself.

There were small streams, gravel bottomed, with sweet cool water to drink and splash on our faces. We followed one of them downhill to a small waterfall and from there to a bigger river, where the water ran so white that we christened it Milk River at once.

"Why *is* it that color?" I asked.

"Kaolin, I expect." Katie lay flat on the grass and reached over, scrabbling with her fingers until she had freed a ball of sticky mud from the river bank. "Look at it. Beautiful stuff." She rolled it into a ball, pushed her thumb into it, and quickly turned it into the rough shape of a cup. "But almost too fat to use by itself. It needs to be mixed with fine sand." She squashed the cup back into a ball of clay and tossed it into the water.

There was an echoing splash downstream as a large fish leapt from the water and fell back. If we had fishing poles and lines, I thought idly . . . Katie rubbed her clay-whitened hands on her coveralls and we walked on until, about an hour later, we came out on a sandy bank. Below it, the river spilled into a wide water meadow, lavishly sprinkled with flowers—yellow, white, and blood red. The river spread out in meanders and marshes and then, presumably, fell away to the lower ground beyond. We could see no more. Beyond the water meadow was only tree-tangled mist.

We collapsed on the ground, falling back onto the sweet-smelling turf, letting the sun and soft wind play over our city-whitened bodies. I shut my eyes and breathed the flower-laden air. I ran my hands over the soft grass. Beside me, Benta turned her face and I saw in its shining that she was happy again.

"It's not real," Rich muttered, over and over, like an incantation. And in my own head a small voice worried at me, the way a piece of grit can worry your foot. An echo of Rich. *It's not real. None of this is real. They're reading your mind and giving you what you long for most. Don't get taken in.*

One by one, we fell asleep and came softly out of sleep to find ourselves on the gray couches in the gray room. In a wordless peace we walked down the deserted passage to the changing rooms and got out of our coveralls and into the brilliant motley uniform of the unemployed.

At the door, we came face to face with a group of ten eager youngsters. "You've been playing The Game?" one of them asked.

We nodded.

"Is it exciting? Can you tell us what happens?"

None of us had the words to explain. "You'll have to see for yourself," Scylla said at last. "I expect it's different for everyone."

I remembered hearing the same response from the girl to whom I had spoken on *our* first visit to Barton Oaks. I had thought her reticence was the result of a rule or a matter of etiquette. But now I knew. She hadn't told me because there just weren't any *words*. As we walked home from the subway I realized that I had left my anger and my disbelief somewhere down in the water meadow.

Even Rich was changed. Some magic in that quiet sleep

had overcome his doubts. When we picked up a germ from a miserable old woman who swapped us a load of moth-eaten wool for some of Scylla's paintings, he was frantic at his inability to treat us, since none of the expensive antibiotics he was used to were available to us. He began to concentrate on folk medicine, which treated sickness with herbs such as feverfew and garlic, healall and parsley. He and Katie developed a friendly partnership between medicine and botany, aided by the practical Benta.

Meanwhile Paul, assisted by the rest of us, extended and refined the map of the Game territory, marking in color everything we had found that might be a clue.

"Next time we go back," Katie remarked, after we had argued ourselves to a standstill one morning, "I'd like to make a real pot with that clay and see if I can fire it."

"*If* you could make a fire," Trent pointed out.

"Exactly."

"But they won't let us take anything through, even a lighter or a single match."

"People must have made fire in the old days, before lighters, I mean. Karen, do you know how they did it?"

"It began with wild fire, from a lightning strike or volcanic activity. People started a fire from that and kept it going afterward. If they had to travel, they stored hot coals in a pot until they could remake the fire in their new home."

"Suppose there weren't any lightning storms? Or volcanoes?" Katie asked.

"A hand drill could generate enough heat to ignite very dry rotten wood or straw, I suppose. If you could rotate it fast enough. And striking a flint on steel, of course. That was used for centuries. But you have to have steel—or maybe iron would do."

"And flints."

"We'll see if there's anything useful on fire-making and firing pottery in the old library."

Meanwhile Scylla unraveled the moth-eaten cloth we'd exchanged and began spinning it into new thread. She bullied Brad and Trent into building her a frame loom. She strung her threads on it and found a way of lifting half the threads and leaving the rest behind, so that she could push a shuttle of thread through and beat it down. It wasn't long before she was able to make good fabric, and out of the fabric, new clothing.

"It would be fun to build a loom on the bank above the water meadow," she said dreamily one day.

"You talk as if the Game country were a place to live, not just to find clues in," Karen teased her.

"We're all doing it, aren't we? Building fires, making pots. And Rich and Katie looking for healing herbs."

"Only none of the herbs are like any we've seen or read about. It's as if the Game world was a foreign country!" Katie frowned.

We did try to make fire in the misty land but, whether we were stupid or the materials were too wet with dew, we could never manage it. It didn't really matter. The days were always warm and sunny. There were nuts to eat and, in any case, we were never allowed to stay there long enough to get really hungry.

It had been spring when we left the Government school for our DA in the grimy city. So little grew in the gritty streets that we were hardly aware of the seasons. The days just grew longer, the city air more oppressive. Then it grew slowly cooler. It seemed to drizzle constantly. That was all. The warehouse grew cold and we were thankful for all the cloth that Scylla had woven, piling squares of stuff on our beds at night and wrapping them around our shoulders like shawls during the day.

Winter made the unchanging summer of the Game country even more wonderful. The sun shone, the flowers never withered, the nuts were always ripe. We explored the slopes below the water meadow and discovered that far to the south lay a huge lake or inland freshwater sea whose extent we could not guess, since the water met the sky in a blur of misty blue with no hint of a far shore. Back in the city, Brad began to read about boatmaking, and he and Trent used the wood-working equipment to make models.

We lived for The Game. Every moment in that place was magic. Every day in the dingy city was only a preparation for a return to Barton Oaks. Hunting for clues and looking forward to a prize was no longer important. Only Rich and Paul continued to pore over the map, trying to wring some answers from it. What *will* happen if we answer the riddle and win the prize? I wondered.

"Don't get it right," I begged Paul and Rich. "We won't

be allowed to go back." But they just laughed at me.

"It's much more likely that we are only allowed a certain number of tries at The Game, win or lose. Then that'll be that." Paul shrugged.

"Don't say that! They can't take it from us now."

My heart echoed Benta's cry. It was worse for her, of course. And Rich. They'd given up more for The Game than the rest of us had.

It grew colder and darker. We waited for another summons to Barton Oaks. A week went by. And another. Trent and Paul began to fight again, and Rich to scorn.

"They're playing games with us. Mind games, depriving us of pleasure, like rats in a trap, watching us—"

"Shut up! Shut up!" I screamed and went for him. Brad pulled me away and held me tight until I stopped crying. A year ago, that would have been comfort enough. Now it was meaningless. All I could think of was a maze with us running back and forth and a great eye watching us from above.

Spring once more. I actually saw a bunch of daffodils in a worker's flower shop across the street from the border of our DA. I longed to run across the street and stand with my nose against the glass, warming my soul with their sunny color. As I stood staring, two youths in red-and-gold motley appeared from the shadows, lounging against the grimy brickwork.

"Come on," one of them called. "What are you afraid of? I'll buy you a daff if you come over here."

The other laughed raucously, and I saw a glint of steel in his belt. I turned and ran back to the safety of our home, with the brightness of the daffodils in my mind, forgetting all about the thread for which I was supposed to scrounge. I was weeping inside for the touch of a daffodil. A single daffodil.

I mourned for that image of spring and sunshine until another envelope appeared. Another invitation to Barton Oaks! Another chance to go through the door into a world, however unreal, where golden flowers bloomed so lavishly that it was hard not to trample on them as one walked. We had not been forgotten after all.

Joyfully I sank back into the familiar gray chair. I shut my eyes. Willingly I relaxed. And dreamed. I had never dreamed before. It had always been an instantaneous transfer. Afterward, when it seemed important, I tried to remember the dream, but I never could. There were no visual images to hang on to. Only a sense of movement and pressure. Of time passing. How can one dream of time passing?

Then the dream was over. Before I even opened my eyes I knew that something had gone wrong.

SEVEN

May 2155. Second Level

I felt horrible, achy and weak, as if I had just had the flu. I couldn't even open my eyes and, when I tried to move, I felt as if I were tied down. I gave up, groaned and drifted into sleep. I had no idea how much later it was when I woke again. The others were just stirring as I sat up and stared around me.

"Where on earth *are* we? This is like nothing we've seen before."

"I thought that was a gray sky up there, but it isn't, is it?"

Brad stood up and his head banged against the "sky" with a hollow plastic sound. "Ouch! We're inside . . . something."

At his words, this new Game world came into focus. We were in a bubble-like house of semi-transparent, whitish plastic, furnished with ten couches, not unlike the ones we had lain on back at Barton Oaks—the ones we were *still* lying on, if Rich's theories were correct and this was all an electronic dream.

"Let's get out of here. Where's the door? I suppose there *is* a door." Brad felt the walls.

We panicked momentarily at the thought of being confined in this cramped white egg, before noticing the handle to a door that was itself invisible. Brad and Katie struggled with it, tugging it, turning it. Finally, swung through one hundred and eighty degrees, the handle released the door, which swung quietly outward, spilling us onto spiky desert grass.

"Where are we *this* time? Any idea, Paul?"

Paul looked around. "Isn't that the mesa over there? Or one very like it? But with this overcast it's hard to tell where north is."

"It's never been overcast before."

"I think I can see the line of the forest"—Katie squinted her eyes—"so north should be *that* way."

"We're almost bound to come to Milk River, and we should be able to find the water meadow from there," added Scylla comfortingly.

We set off toward the misty line of the forest. It was only later that we thought about how odd our behavior was, turning our backs on the mysterious translucent bubble. And only much later were we to realize why.

Even through the cloud cover the sun was hot, and at first walking was difficult. The sandy soil under the short sharp-edged grass was soft and uneven beneath our feet. Our toes were continually being caught in tangles of shallow roots. Small flies rose in thick clouds and buzzed irritatingly around our ankles. When they found our ankles protected by boots and coveralls, they rose higher and discovered the tender skin of our hands and wrists.

"Ugh! Let's get out of this place! Come on." Trent doubled his speed, striding between the grass clumps. I found it hard to keep up, as if I had weights in my boots.

"Ease up, Trent," Rich gasped.

"Told you to exercise more." Brad grinned.

"You *are* going too fast," I added, and Trent slowed down.

"Oh, well, if you're *all* out of condition . . ." But I noticed that he was breathing very hard and that sweat was running down his forehead.

The sun was shining sulkily through the clouds in the southwest before we got to the end of the grassland and found ourselves under the comforting shade of the big trees.

"Let's rest. I'm beat." I sank to the grass.

"Me too."

"But we've hardly been any distance at all, less than six miles."

"I know. But Lisse's right. I'm done."

I lay back thankfully in the cool grass. What was the matter with me? I felt tired right through to my bones. And my eyes . . .

"There's something odd about this place. Or maybe it's the weather." Scylla's slow voice echoed my thoughts.

I sat up and stared at her. "Like . . . as if the brightness had gone?"

She nodded. "As if someone had painted a gray wash over all the brilliant colors. It's not the same."

"Any idea why?" Brad asked, but the others shook their heads.

We forced ourselves to get up and walk on through the

trees, hoping to find the familiar place above the water meadows before nightfall. It seemed farther away than before and it was twilight before we came to a stream running downhill toward the river, which must flow somewhere below us. I knelt and splashed my face and gulped handfuls of water. It was surprisingly cold, enough to make my teeth ache, and it had a metallic, not unpleasant, taste to it.

"The water's refreshing. Goodness, I'm thirsty. And hungry too. Do you see any nut trees, Benta?"

"Why yes, all those big smooth-barked ones are bearing nuts."

I looked in the grass. "But there aren't any."

"Up there, silly." She pointed at small green clusters among the leaves. "But they won't be ripe for months."

"That's very odd." Katie stared up at the trees. "We can't possibly be in a different climatic zone. Why were the nuts ripe every other time and not now?"

"Perhaps we've been brought into The Game at a different season," I suggested.

"That's it, of course." Scylla's deep voice was relieved. "That's why it looks different. And the plague of flies, when they never bothered us before. It's a different time of year, that's all."

"Though that doesn't account for why we feel so tired, does it?"

No one had an answer. We trudged downhill. The ground was rough and my ankles ached. Twilight crept through the forest. The shadows of tree trunks fell in bars across the short turf, so that they were like steps leading slowly downward, one by one. We had to be careful not to trip over the tree roots that snaked along the ground.

"It'll be night in a minute," Paul said regretfully. "Then they'll zap us back to Barton Oaks."

"We're still there," said Rich, predictably.

"Oh, do shut up," Scylla snapped, which surprised Rich so much that he did.

We emerged from a thick stand of nut trees onto a bluff high above the water meadows through which the river meandered, considerably to the east of our familiar stopping place.

It was a splendid place to camp, though, with dry sandy soil that sloped to the crumbling edge of the bluff. From it we could see the march of great trees to east and west, while to the north layers of ancient river banks led down in a series of terraces to the present valley bottom. We had a bird's-eye view of the pattern of its meanders through the flower-strewn water meadows.

The evening was far from silent. The air shimmered with the hum, creak, and whine of night insects, and the bushes along the bluff were alive with the twitter of small birds.

"Oh, listen! What was that?" Benta's voice trembled. In the silence we all heard again the strange, yawning cry of a larger animal.

"Do you suppose it's dangerous?" I whispered.

"There aren't any wild animals left. They're all in zoos." Katie's matter-of-fact voice was comforting.

But then the cry came again. "So what's that, huh? Come on, know-it-all. What was that?" Rich's voice rose hysterically. "I could kill you people for dragging me into this. . . ."

"Cheer up, scaredy-cat. You know you're just lying on a couch at Barton Oaks. None of this is real."

At Trent's imitation of Rich's pompous tones, we all laughed. But our laughter soon died away. The sun had dropped behind the trees to the west. A cool wind shivered through the leaves. It felt very real.

"Maybe we should gather wood for a fire. And think about a shelter."

"They'll probably zap us back to Barton Oaks before we have a chance to get a fire started, but . . . all right. Why don't we? It'll be fun." Scylla's cheerful voice encouraged us into movement.

We separated, looking for fallen branches of small, dead trees that we could drag back to the bluff. Most of the wood was still green and supple, hard to break with our bare hands, and between the ten of us we managed to collect only a meager supply of firewood.

Then Brad had us search for a flat piece of wood and a straight pointed stick to use as a fire-drill. He rejected five or six before we found something he thought might do. We sat around and watched him rub his palms to and fro so that the stick twirled like a drill, point down against the flat piece of wood.

"I think it's getting warm," Benta encouraged him after a time.

"Not as warm as my palms are. Anyone else want to have a try?"

We took turns, spinning the drill between our hands, trying to go fast enough, bearing down on the stick so that its friction against the other piece of wood might be enough to start a fire.

It began to rain. Not a downpour, just a slow, persistent drizzle. The firewood we had so painfully acquired began to get wet and we pushed it under bushes to keep off the rain. I put the pulpy wood with which we had hoped to start the fire in the knee pocket of my coveralls.

"This is hopeless," said Alden at last, tossing aside the drill and blowing on his hot palms.

"But we're getting wetter and wetter. Why don't you *do* something?"

"It's all in your mind, Rich, remember?"

"If you say that once more . . ." Rich swung at Trent. Katie caught his wrist and twisted it. Rich thumped to the ground.

"I think you've broken my hand," he moaned.

"Stop it, all of you!" Scylla shouted. "Get the biggest boughs and we'll make a lean-to. Something to keep off the worst of the wet."

We huddled together inside our makeshift shelter. There was not quite enough room for ten of us, and as the wind rose and whipped the rain, now a genuine downpour, under the open ends, those of us on the outside grew wetter.

"We'll probably all develop pneumonia." Rich sneezed.

"They'd never let anything happen to us." Katie's voice was confident.

"I sure hope you're right. But who are 'they' anyway? We've only seen one human being at Barton Oaks. Maybe the whole thing is run by robots. We know *they* don't have any real concern for us."

"They *must*. They can't have just left us here." Benta began to cry and I struggled to free an arm to put around her. "I wish I were home. Oh, why did you have to think of me? Why couldn't you have left me in peace?" She shrugged my arm off her shoulder. I tried not to cry. Benta rejecting me was worse than the cold, the wet, the fear.

"Anyway, Rich, if we're not really here, if it's all in our minds, how can we possibly catch pneumonia?" Trent was still on the same track.

"If we get pneumonia, we'll be getting it in the real world too. Ugh, the rain's running down my neck. And my throat's beginning to tickle."

"Take my place, Rich. It's quite cozy in the middle." I couldn't help feeling sorry for him. After all, I thought, he hasn't roughed it the way we have. I couldn't help smiling at a sudden vision of Rich in his comfortably furnished doctor's office, with armchairs and couch, soft music, and an obedient robot-nurse.

The night was very long. I dozed occasionally, awakening with a jolt when someone cautiously moved a cramped arm or leg, or when the position of my own body became too uncomfortable to bear. Each time I woke I expected to find myself back at Barton Oaks, warm and dry, the comfortable reclining chair at my back. I willed it to happen. I tried holding my breath. I pinched myself awake. Nothing worked. There was no possible doubt. We were stuck in this suddenly disagreeable episode of The Game.

Was the whole thing an elaborate joke? Were "they" playing with us, sucking us into a joyful acceptance of The Game, only to snatch it away? If so, it was a very expensive joke. Ridiculously expensive.

In my mind, during that long night, I ran through everything that the Manager had told us. He'd talked about arcade games, video games. . . . I remembered Brad's achievements with computer games when we were kids at school, exploring the rooms of castles and dungeons, each booby-trapped in more ingenious ways, each crowded with opponents of ever-increasing strength and subtlety. *Increasing subtlety.* That was it!

The rain stopped shortly before dawn and the sun rose palely on a land smoking with mist. I crept out of the lean-to without disturbing the others. Ouch! I was stiff! And chilly, my coveralls wet all down the right side from the night's rainfall.

I began to jog westward along the bluffs, hoping to find the place where we had stayed during our previous Game experiences. I swung my arms and tried to think warm. After almost two miles I had still not come upon the place. I turned and jogged back, the sun warming my front and drying the damp patches on my coveralls.

The others had wakened and were standing in a huddle, like a collection of individuals waiting at a bus stop. Not like a *group* anymore.

Scylla was trying to generate some energy. "We can hunt for flints and start a fire that way."

"We don't really *need* a fire, Scylla." Brad had his own ideas. "Raw fish is perfectly—"

"No way! Oh, for a little hot chicken soup. My throat—"

"Why don't you just pipe down, Rich, before I make your sore throat worse?"

"What's happened to you all? You sound just awful!"

"Lisse, where have you *been*?"

"Jogging. I looked for our old place. But I couldn't find it."

"How far did you go?"

"Almost two miles, I think."

"Who cares? When are those idiots going to bring us back?"

"I don't know that they are, Rich. Not yet. I've been thinking. Do you remember those computer games at school, Brad? As soon as you won at a certain level you were automatically bumped up to the next and harder level. It was the same world, but the rules were different, tougher."

Brad and Scylla saw what I was getting at right away. "It's a good sign, really, isn't it? We've passed the first level. Now we're on to the second."

"I see," said Alden thoughtfully, while the others still stared, puzzled. "We're being challenged with a more difficult environment."

"And we're not making much of a go of this second level, are we? Sitting grouching over a bit of rain! All right, everyone. We'll show them." Brad's face lit up. "What's the first thing we should do?"

"Get something to eat," Paul said. He tended to sulk and this was about the first thing he'd said since nightfall, so I was glad when the others agreed.

"Right. We'll gather and we'll fish. There must be some berries and roots fit to eat. Be very careful. Katie, you'd better go with one group and you, Benta, with the other. You should be able to identify species. Rich, would you recognize a poisonous substance?"

"Not till you started foaming at the mouth and rolling on the ground."

"That's not funny, Rich."

"Well, don't eat funguses anyway. They're tricky. The symptoms don't show up for a while, and then it's too late. Avoid anything bitter or acrid . . . oh, I don't know." He waved his hands helplessly.

"We can use pointed sticks for digging," suggested Katie. "And if you should find a really good berry bush, yell and we'll come running."

"What group are you going to join, Brad?"

He stuck out his jaw and looked obstinate. "I'm going to stay here and get that stupid fire going."

Benta went east with Trent and Karen, Katie followed the way I had jogged earlier, taking Alden and Paul with her. I gave Brad the piece of fire starter I had saved in the knee pocket of my coveralls and set out with Scylla to find a way down from the bluffs to the water meadow below.

"Coming, Rich?" I asked.

He shivered and I saw panic in his eyes. He looked somehow smaller today. He shook his head.

"Oh, come on, Rich." I put a hand on his shoulder and for a moment I thought he'd break down and come. But then he shrugged my hand off, so I turned and followed Scylla down the bluff to the valley floor.

White and gold flowers lay above wide shiny leaves in an almost solid mat over the water. When we pulled on them, the whole plant came up, exposing plump white tubers.

"What do you think?" I asked.

"Well, at least the water isn't polluted."

I began to laugh. It was so comical. Here we were in a world as new—even if it were imaginary—as Paradise, and we were afraid to eat in case we were poisoned. It was ironic.

"Oh, well, here goes nothing." I broke one of the tubers in two. It snapped cleanly like a fresh carrot. It was white inside. I touched my tongue cautiously to the broken surface.

"Do be careful, Lisse. What's it like?"

"Sweet." I scraped a little pulp into my mouth with my front teeth and held it there, ready to spit it out if it felt wrong. I chewed it. Definitely sweet. Pleasant. I swallowed.

Scylla's face made me laugh. "It really does taste like food, you know. It must be loaded with starch. Good filling stuff. Let's fill our pockets. If I'm still all right by the time we get back to the others, we can be sure it's safe to eat."

We tried to get close to open water, but the mat of water plants shook under our feet. In our clumsy attempts to find a foothold we startled a clutch of funny frog-like creatures, which jumped from the leaves in every direction. Scylla caught one easily. It wriggled slimily in her hands and its eyes goggled frantically.

"*Is* it a frog?" she asked uncertainly. "It doesn't look like the ones in the stream behind the school, does it? People used to eat frogs' legs. I read it somewhere. . . ." Her voice trailed off.

"We won't, though, will we? Even if it is."

"No, of course not." She opened her hand and the creature leapt downward and vanished beneath the leaves.

We made our way delicately back to firm ground and, after walking under the bluff for a while, came to a place where the river curved toward us, eating away at the sandy bank, running clear, with no marsh plants to get in our way. We lay on our fronts on the bank and stared into the water. Large, shadowy shapes lurked near the bottom. I thought they were stones at first, until one moved its tail.

"Huge fish," Scylla whispered. "That's not like eating frogs' legs, is it?"

"Not a bit. But how do we catch one?"

"We need a line and a bait. And a hook, of course."

A line. I looked down at my coveralls, seamed perfectly from top to bottom, with not so much as a loose thread. Then Scylla's hair caught my eye. It reached almost to her waist, copper-colored and coarse.

She saw my look. "All right. In the interests of the common good. But I'll pull them myself, thank you. How many do you need?"

"Let's try five for a start. I'll braid them. If this works we should start saving your combings. We could start a whole industry based on your hair."

She looked at me seriously. "You sound as if you think we'll be here a long time."

"No, no. I didn't mean that. I was only joking."

She pulled out five hairs, grimacing fiercely, and I sat with them across my knee, plaiting them into a thin but strong line. While I worked, Scylla looked around.

"This bush has tough-looking thorns. If I can tear off a piece of bark with the thorn you'll have—ouch—a hook. What do you think?"

Trying to fasten the thorn to our tiny line was infuriating, and even worse was fastening a grub to the whole thing, but I got it done at last and Scylla lowered the line into the water. I could see the grub straighten and curl and I could almost feel the shiver of interest from the big fish below.

"Slowly," I whispered. "Go slowly."

Scylla stuck her tongue out at me and concentrated, carefully lowering the line. The fish gulped and the grub vanished.

"Oh, careful. If the barb breaks . . ."

The fish suddenly turned. Its tail thrashed and she hauled the line out of the water with the fish on the end. It was as long as my arm, spotted orange and green. Mouth agape, it shook itself, and in the instant that it went free I flung myself into the water and caught its slippery body, my fingers groping blindly for the gills. I floundered out of the water and fell backward on dry land with the fish flapping on my chest.

"Got it. Got it. Oh, do something!"

"Quick. Put it down." Scylla stood over me, a rock in her hand.

I rolled out of the way and shut my eyes as the rock came down. I hadn't really believed we could do it, not without proper tackle. Now we will have real hooks, I thought, as I picked the huge creature up by its gill flaps. Hooks made out of fish bones. One thing would lead to another. Always getting better. If only Brad had got the fire going.

As we climbed to the top of the bluffs, I imagined a spiral of blue smoke rising in the still air, the tang of burning wood. It would be horrible cutting up a raw fish, but if we could bake it first it would come apart easily. Also the river had been cold and I was starting to shiver, in spite of the sun.

There was no fire. No Brad. Only Rich, sitting basking with his back against a tree.

"*Rich!*"

He opened his eyes. "Hmm?"

"Where did Brad go?"

"How should I know?"

"All right, master surgeon. This is where you earn your keep. You're going to have to cut this up."

Rich looked down in horror. "Me? That? What with, pray tell?"

"I don't know. A sharp stick. Maybe a stone, slate or something like that."

"I couldn't cut up a raw fish."

"D'you want to eat today?"

"Come *on*."

"I mean it. No work, no food."

I slid into the bushes, leaving them arguing, and got out of my clothes, wrung them as dry as I could, shook them out and put them on again. By the time I got back the fish was a mangled mess, but there were still some good-sized chunks of it laid out on leaves. I picked up a shred. Pink flesh, firm and beautiful. But raw . . .

I closed my eyes. It tasted cool and delicate, quite unfishy. My stomach clamored for more. "Scylla, it's all right. It's *good*."

The other groups returned before we had eaten more than our share. Their mouths were blue with berry juice and their hands were full. Fish, roots, and berries. It would have been a great meal if it had only been cooked. Although it filled my stomach, I still felt chilly.

"And I came across something almost as important as food." Katie fished in her pocket. "A seam of chalk."

"So Scylla can draw more murals? How fascinating! How useful!" Rich's eyebrows went up.

"Chalk commonly contains nodules of flint, like these." Katie held up two roundish rocks, each the size of a large potato. She was grinning broadly. "Once we've learned how to break them into flakes, we'll have knives and scrapers, even saws and sickles. And . . ." She struck the two stones a glancing blow, one against the other, "and definitely fire!"

By that evening we had constructed a proper lean-to of logs, with sides as well as a back thatched roughly with bundles of grass to shed the rain. A fire burned in its entrance, a fire Brad and Scylla decided to keep burning as long as we stayed: we would take turns watching over it through the nights.

"Nights?" Rich screamed. "How long are we going to be stuck in this godforsaken place?"

"I want to go home," Benta whispered. "This place is hateful."

"No, it's not. It's . . ."

"Well, what is it, Lisse? What's so special about this place?"

They were all silent, looking at me, waiting for me to answer Benta's question. Benta's challenge.

I looked around, trying to recapture the delight of those earlier visits to the Game country: the clear, invigorating air, the kindliness of the sun, the sense of excitement and discovery that had drawn us in so that we went to extravagant lengths to fit ourselves for the adventure. But instead I saw sopping vegetation and felt the ache in my bones and the chill of clothes not ever quite dry, the discomfort of the sleepless night.

Benta watched my face. "It's different now, isn't it? When you have to *stay*. When you don't go home to a good meal and a warm bed."

"It's still better than the city," I burst out. "We can go where we want. There's no Designated Area. No thought police. No gangs."

"No anything. It's not better for me." She shook her head. "Nor for Rich. It's not *fair*."

"Come," said Scylla gently. "The fish is beautifully cooked and the tubers we baked in the embers are ready. We'll feel better after a hot meal. Remember, it's only a test."

"For how long? That's the question, isn't it? And suppose that after this level there's another and another. And each of them is worse. Think about that."

"Shut up and eat, Trent, and try not to be quite so negative." Brad raked a tuber from the embers and broke it open. Its sweet fragrance filled the air and we forgot our fears and quarrels for the time being as we filled our stomachs.

It rained almost without intermission for the next six days and nights. Our time was spent in finding and preparing enough food and keeping dry, keeping the fire going. That first spark had caught only because the pulpy wood starter had stayed in my pocket, next to my skin, during the first rainy night. The ground squelched beneath our feet, rain dripping from the branches. If the fire went out, we knew we could never get it going again. At night, two of us stayed awake, in case one should fall asleep and let the fire die.

"If only it would stop raining," Rich grumbled.

"Perhaps it's a kind of monsoon season," I said hopefully. "Once it's over things'll be different."

But it went on raining. Each day of struggling to dry wood and find enough food was followed by a night of chilly discomfort as we crowded into our shelter and tried to sleep on ground only a little padded with layers of more or less dry grass. I caught a cold that seemed to settle in my chest. I lay awake on the seventh night, trying not to cough and wake the others, wondering how long this phase would last. What did they expect of us, the people at Barton Oaks? In the first phase of The Game, they had pulled us back so quickly, often long before we wanted to leave. Now it seemed as if we had been forgotten.

My chest hurt each time I drew a breath. I stifled another cough. Perhaps the Manager of Barton Oaks had gone out to lunch and all this discomfort, six days of it, was taking place in the time between soup and pie.

On the other hand, suppose something had happened in the city? Suppose one of the pamphlet-printing groups had actually brought off a revolution? Perhaps Barton Oaks had been abandoned. Perhaps our wired-up bodies were right now lying helpless on the gray couches in the gray room behind the secret door. Perhaps they would lie there till they rotted. What would become of the essential *us* then? Would we vanish, and this imaginary land with us?

My head throbbed and I felt quite wretchedly ill. I longed to be at home, curled up on my dry mattress in our warehouse castle, with a pile of Scylla's woven shawls to keep me warm, with hot soup or cocoa to soothe my chest. How wonderful a hot drink would be right now.

I fell into a feverish dream-filled sleep in which I was tied down to a couch with electric wires running from my body to a computer terminal. Every once in a while Rich would turn on a switch and a jolt would shake my body.

"Make him stop," I yelled to Brad and Scylla, but they only smiled. "Benta," I screamed and woke with a start, my cry echoing in my ears. It was daylight. The sun was shafting palely between rain-heavy clouds. The others were already up and moving around. I was lying close to the fire, which blazed fiercely. I could feel its heat on my face, although my body was like ice.

Scylla brought me a gourd full of hot water with some herbs floating in it.

"What is it?" I was touchy and suspicious, my dream fresh in my memory.

"Just herb tea. Rich thinks it'll help bring down your fever."

"I don't want it. Rich wants to hurt me—" I stopped at the expression on Scylla's face. That had been a dream, hadn't it? Or was *this* the dream? I remembered Paul's story of the archbishop and the grasshopper, but my head was too muddled to work it out. I allowed Scylla to lift me up and help me drink the bitter contents of the gourd. The warmth inside me was comforting, but my head spun sickeningly and I was thankful to be able to lie down again.

When I came slowly to the surface again it was noon.

Tendrils of mist were steaming up from the wet ground. The others were outside, talking softly, but suddenly I could hear every word.

"I think her fever's down but there's a risk of pneumonia."

"Rich, there can't be. This isn't *real*. You've said so a thousand times. They *have* to bring us back if there's any danger," Paul argued.

"Can we be sure of that?"

"They always did before."

"This time's different, isn't it? We agreed. A new phase. Perhaps we're allowed to be in life-threatening situations. . . ."

They all began to talk at once then, their voices raised. Benta said, "Hush, you'll wake her."

"There's something on my mind," Brad said softly in the silence that followed. I could still hear every word, as clearly as if he were whispering into my ear. "I don't believe this *is* a new phase of The Game. That was a plausible idea at first. But it's been a *week*. We've all lost weight. We're not sleeping as well as we should. We have no change of clothes, no support at all—"

"Are you saying we're stuck here *forever*?" Paul's voice was high.

His question seemed to echo back and forth across the valley. Forever . . . Ever . . . Ever.

"That *is* what you're saying, isn't it, Brad?" Trent broke the uneasy silence. "That this is real. That The Game's over and *this* is the prize."

"Some prize." Rich began to laugh hysterically.

"Shut up, Rich," everyone said automatically.

Brad went on. "It's the only logical solution, isn't it? We felt different from the first moment we got here, didn't we? Even though we haven't talked a lot about it. The other place—The Game—was a kind of ideal, where the sun always shone and the insects didn't bite. This is reality. When we don't eat we get hungry. When we're wet we get chilled. Nobody *can* turn a switch to bring us back, because it *is* real. Lisse's ill and if she gets any worse she'll die and I know, if we were still playing The Game, they'd have brought us back by now."

"Two questions then." Karen's logical voice calmed the sudden beating of my heart at the possibility of death. "Where are we? And for how long? Is the prize for winning The Game a vacation in glorious wherever-this-is? Or are we here for life?"

As I sank back into the dark pit of my illness, Karen's questions jabbed at me like a needle. Where *are* we? And are we here for life?

EIGHT

June 2155. Galaxy Game

Whether because of Rich's herb drinks or my natural resilience, my fever broke that day and within a week I was almost as fit as before. We held a council the day Rich finally pronounced me well. "Ways and Means," Scylla called it.

"Before we start going off in all directions, I'd like to discuss the basic idea behind The Game." Rich still managed a pompous couch-side manner in spite of uncombed hair, unshaven chin, and weather-stained coveralls.

"Do go ahead." Scylla's face was solemn, though I could see from the sparkle in her eyes that she got a kick out of Rich's manner.

"Thank you. Perhaps because I arrived later than the rest of you—"

"Except for me," Benta put in.

"Yes, of course. Except for Benta." Rich frowned and began again, as if he were lecturing an invisible audience. "They say that the newcomer sees most of the game . . . in this case THE GAME, ha-ha, and it seems clear to me that our experience here is an example of aversion therapy."

"What on earth are you talking about?"

"Bear with me, Alden. First of all there is the build-up to make you *want* to play The Game. There is the secrecy and then the sense of being chosen. Afterward you experience a series of paradise-like events, during which you may travel freely, make new discoveries, all the things that are impossible back home. Yet at the same time you are protected against sordid reality—falling off a mesa, eating poisonous berries, and so on—by the management at Barton Oaks, whom you equate with the Government."

"Rich, isn't this all rather pointless?"

"I'm not finished. Suddenly the scenario changes. Your escape from reality is no longer attractive. You are wet, cold, hungry. You are ill. You begin to long for the amenities of the city from which, just a short time ago, you were happy to escape. Aversion therapy. Come on, all of you, admit it . . . you'd be thankful to find yourself back there, wouldn't you? In spite of the dirt, the crowding, the lack of freedom? Wouldn't one of Scylla's potato-and-turnip stews taste wonderful? And what price a night's sleep on a good mattress?"

Rich smiled smugly. We sat silently, taking it in. I felt the way I had, years and years before, knowing for sure that Santa Claus wasn't real. Only this was worse.

"Are you saying that The Game keeps the unemployed under control by making them grateful for what they've got? On the principle of anything being better than this?" Alden's voice was skeptical and I felt better. Maybe there *was* a Santa Claus after all.

"But it does hold together," Karen said slowly. "It's a bit more subtle than I would have expected of a Government kept in power by the thought police, but — "

"It's bunk!" Benta's face was flushed. "There's a hole in your theory you could drop a cow through, Rich. You and me. Why should *we* have been subjected to this aversion therapy? I was totally happy helping Dad on the farm. It's all I ever wanted to do. And I suppose you were as contented in your father's practice? Well, then."

"If you're so clever, Benta, why don't *you* explain what's going on?"

"I'm not clever, Rich. I've just got common sense and it tells me your idea isn't logical. Either we've been given a vacation somewhere as a prize for whatever we did right in The Game or . . . or we've emigrated."

"Emigrated? I *see*. Yes, to cut down on the unemployment population in the big centers. That makes some sense, though it *still* doesn't account for Rich and Benta. And where *are* we? I didn't think there was anywhere left on Earth to emigrate *to*."

"The middle of Australia, perhaps," said Paul vaguely. "Or Tibet."

Brad stood up and stretched. He never could bear to sit still for long. "Does it matter? All this talk. The important thing is that we're here and we've got to make the best of it. Get rid of the chinks in the lean-to. Find something better to eat than fish and roots. A better fireplace. It's crazy to have to stay up nights to tend it. And we need more clothes and some bedding — "

"I've been thinking about that," Scylla interrupted.

"Now that the rain's finally stopped, I think we should build a loom, find fibers from grasses or trees, or animals, if there are any, and start to weave fabric."

"*Weave* fabric? That's ridiculous. We'll only be here for a week or two at the most. . . ."

"We're not here at all. It's all in our minds—"

"Well, I think we should. . . ."

The sense of being a team, which had held us together through our dangerous early days in the city, began to fall apart in front of my eyes. Scylla saw it too and tried to pull us together.

"Let's act on the assumption that we *have* been transplanted to another country to make a new beginning. What's the harm in it? Even if we're proved wrong we will have spent our days constructively."

"It may even be part of The Game," I suggested. "To test us in crisis."

But, though Scylla cajoled and Brad bullied, Rich, Alden, and Trent refused to believe that this new situation was going to last.

"What are you going to do, then?" Brad snapped.

"Just wait for them to zap us back to Barton Oaks." Trent looked more obstinate than usual. "It's going to happen, you know. And you're all going to look pretty stupid with your plans for looms and houses."

It wouldn't have been so bad if all they did was wait, but they didn't. What actually happened was that the three dissidents hung around, getting in everyone else's way and criticizing. There were angry words and Trent and Paul started fighting again.

The rest of us decided that the most pressing need was a source of protein other than fish. We needed fur and leather too. There was no arguing even though, emotionally, we would rather have been vegetarians.

"There are bound to be small creatures around," Benta said. "I can't think why we haven't seen them. We should look for traces and then make traps."

"Traces?" We stared.

"Droppings. Pathways through the undergrowth. Bushes that have been grazed on."

We divided into two groups and set off among the trees. Now that we were looking for them, we easily found the traces Benta had described. There were holes in the bole of an ancient nut tree. There was a neat pile of pellets where two tiny pathways crossed. There were traces everywhere, although we never saw a single animal nor heard anything but the chatter of small birds.

"I expect they come out in the evening," said Brad. "We've heard sounds then, haven't we? Only we're always in bed by dark."

"How can we possibly catch them at night? Oh, if only they'd let us bring a flashlight!" I lamented.

"The battery would wear out and where would we get another one? It's easy, actually. We'll use snares, the way we did on the farm."

"I thought farmers used poison."

"Some do. Dad and I used snares and we had rabbit in the pot almost every night."

"Benta, do you know how to skin them and . . . and take out their insides and all that?"

"Of course."

We all sighed with relief. Taking apart a fish with a sharp stone had been horrible enough.

"But only with a good knife," she added.

"It's time I started working on those flints Katie found," Brad said. "As soon as we get back."

We set traps in some of the most-used runs, using plaited strands of Scylla's hair to make running nooses supported by twigs. Back at camp, Brad began to chip at the flint nodules. It was infuriating work, not helped by the rest of us standing around offering advice.

"If any of you want to try, go ahead." Brad stopped to rub his bruised hands.

"It shouldn't be that difficult. After all, early man could do it and he had a much smaller brain capacity." Rich couldn't help getting interested.

"Then you should just about qualify." Brad tossed him a couple of flint nodules. If Rich was actually going to work, none of us would interfere, but watching him destroy his fingers was too much to bear and we turned tactfully away, leaving them to it.

A shout from Katie brought us running to the high bank above the water meadows. On a rock, the strangest creature I'd ever seen was sunning itself. It was as long as my arm, the color of the stone, and spotted with green exactly like lichen. We might have passed dozens like it and never noticed.

"It's a lizard, I think, but nothing like any I've read about." Katie scratched her head. "Look at the way the legs are attached. It's all wrong."

Benta picked it up and its triangular teeth shone wickedly as it hissed and wriggled in her hands.

"Oh, let it go!"

"It's protein, Lisse." Benta expertly broke its neck and I shuddered. "We can skin it, and use the bones as tools if they're not too brittle. And there's a lot of meat on it, far more than on a rabbit."

"Ugh. I don't think I could."

"People eat snakes and lizards all over the world. Once it's cooked you'll never know."

She walked back to camp with a pleased smile, swinging the ugly lizard creature by its tail. Using one of Brad's discarded flint flakes, she managed to skin it. Rich came up as she was skewering its body on a stick.

"I hope you took out all the innards."

"Thanks, Rich. I think I managed." I'd never seen Benta sarcastic before. Come to think of it, I'd never seen Benta kill anything.

"All right, all right. Just make sure no one eats the liver. If there *are* any poisons they're likely to be located there. And here are a couple of flint knives. I knew I could do it."

After that, we had to share the meat with Rich and the other two, even though they hadn't helped. It was annoying, but we couldn't have enjoyed the sweet tender meat if they had gone hungry. It was wonderful eating something other than fish, and Benta was right. Once it was cooked you'd never have known it was lizard.

After our meal, Benta scraped the skin clean and pinned it flat to the wall of the lean-to. She tried to get the meat off the bones, but this was harder. We had not yet found a way of really *boiling* water, since we had no fire-proof containers. All we could do was get it decently hot, and that was a lot of work, dropping hot stones into pots made from an inedible gourd-like plant. Everything we ate had to be either roasted in the ashes or broiled above the flames.

"That's the next thing in our survival plan. Containers."

"What of, Scylla?"

"Tree bark, I suppose."

"Yes, we could soften it in the river and stitch it with fine roots." Benta's face shone with excitement. I was glad she was coming out of her shell and, maybe, forgiving us for our part in bringing her here.

"But that still won't do for cooking," Karen reminded us.

"Remember that time I discovered the bed of kaolin upstream?" Katie got to her feet. "When we called it Milk River and Lisse asked why it was white?"

"So?"

"Pots. We can make pots."

"If we can find the place again. So much seems different this time. . . ."

The bed of clay was there, although there was no trace of our former camp. There were no gouges in the river bank. There was no trace of the pots we'd played at making. It was as if we had never been there. Yet we remembered the place exactly and the clay was still there. It was very puzzling.

We hauled the clay back to camp and experimented. We found that, if we polished the almost-dry pots with a smooth piece of skin or a very round stone, they not only looked better but were more sturdy and fireproof. And we began to decorate them, even though it wasn't in the least necessary.

And now there were animals to put in the pots. The first ones we caught were like short-eared rabbits with strangely bluish fur. Katie was puzzled at not being able to name them, as she had been with the lizard creature.

"Maybe they're mutating from ultraviolet radiation or pollution," Alden suggested, but Rich shook his head.

"These are all alike, not randomly changing. No, Katie, it's a new species."

I looked at the soft purple fur, the glazed eyes that had once been shining with life. "Oh, let's not," I cried. "Suppose they fetch us back to Barton Oaks in a week, couldn't we manage without all this killing?"

"And suppose they don't? You're still as pale as milk and the rest of us are not as fit as when we arrived. We need iron and first-class protein and we're going to get it." Scylla grabbed the limp creatures and gave them to Benta. "Here, and try to keep the skins as whole as possible, will you?"

"Oh, Scylla, how could you be so hard? I thought you were strong, but it's not strength, it's cruelty."

"Lisse, shut up," Benta hissed at me as Scylla turned away.

"So you're against me too!" I ran into the woods until I was out of earshot and cried until I had no tears left.

I went back, ashamed of my outburst, and made myself eat. The stew was delicious, cooked in one of our new pots, with herbs and something like a wild onion, but milder, with a strange cinnamony aftertaste. I could feel the goodness of it coursing through my body and, for the first time since I'd been ill, I slept right through the night. I tried to apologize later, but Scylla wouldn't let me.

"It's all right, Lisse. It wasn't really you. Just fear and fatigue."

Was I afraid? Surely not. Nothing drew me back to the city. And school life was over and there was no going back. I suppose if I was afraid of anything, it was of being abandoned, alone. But not knowing the truth about The Game *was* getting on my nerves. I told myself that when we knew the truth we'd all be less jumpy.

Now we had fire and hot food and, when the next rain came, our lean-to was waterproof. But we desperately needed a change of clothing.

"We can get fiber from plants," Katie suggested. "As well as covering from animal skins, but it'll take ages to collect enough fur to be useful."

"So let's go on a fiber-hunting expedition and build a loom, like I suggested before. I'll teach you all to weave."

"Scylla, you're crazy!" This time it was Alden who overreacted. "We'll only be here a few more days, you'll see."

"What makes you think that? We've been here over three weeks already. Count the notches on the tree. One for every day. Why would they bring us back now?"

"Why not?"

Rich turned on Alden. "You trust the Government to bring us back? You're the one who's crazy."

"But, Rich, *you* don't believe in this place. Aren't we lying in that room in Barton Oaks right now?" Alden sneered.

"I believe they're just playing with us. That's all your Game is—the Government playing games. But I've seen through it." He shook his fist at the empty sky. "You can't fool me."

"Don't, Rich, please!" My voice shook. "Oh, if we only knew. . . ."

Benta put her arm around me and hugged me. "That's a luxury we don't have, Lisse. Knowing. But did we really have it before, back home? I *thought* my life was settled. Then one day—pow, it's all over and I'm on a bus heading for the city. We can't ever *know*. We have to take it . . ."

". . . One day at a time. I know, Benta. I know."

"Come on!" Brad walked up and down, waving his hands. "One day at a time is just surviving. I'm going to live as if we're to be here forever. And I'm going to work my butt off to make this as good a place as possible to live in. And we'll start by building your loom, Scylla, and then we'll try a log cabin. That lean-to's getting pretty rickety."

"A log cabin? Brad, you're as nutty as Scylla!"

"You won't say that when winter comes and you don't have a decent house to keep out the wind and weather or warm clothes to go hunting in."

"*Winter!*" Rich's jaw dropped.

"Brad's right." Karen's voice was thoughtful. "It's June already. Soon it'll be midsummer. After a while it's going to get a lot cooler, how cold we don't know. But we *should* be prepared."

"So *you* don't believe this is a dream, or a vacation. *You* believe we're here for life, don't you?" In spite of myself my voice trembled.

"Yes, Lisse, I think I do. I've been fighting it, but it's the only thing that really makes sense. And I don't mind a bit!"

I nodded, speechless.

"What about you, Karen?" Scylla asked. "Is there somewhere else you would honestly rather be?"

Karen shook her head. "No, not really. But it would have been nice to have been consulted instead of just being zapped here. And I'm curious. Where *are* we? In all the time we've been here we haven't seen a single trace of human habitation, not even an airplane contrail." She looked up at the evening sky, where one star shone. The sun's last rays gilded a small cloud ridge. The sky was otherwise empty.

It was then that Paul made the fatal suggestion. "We've no way of guessing our longitude without clocks, but we ought to be able to make a fair guess at our latitude, if you're curious."

"Of course! By the position of the constellations. If we can remember enough of Astronomy Ten. How about it, Paul? How's your memory of the star charts?" Brad challenged him.

"Good enough for an educated guess. Do you want to stay up tonight and see where we are?"

Even the grouchy three were interested, and that evening, instead of going to bed as soon as the sun set as we had done up till then, the ten of us sat on the sandy bluff above the water meadow, looking across the river and the forest to the horizon. It was wonderfully peaceful, and I remember feeling a bit guilty that, with Earth so overcrowded, we should have this splendid place to ourselves.

The sky slowly darkened and the rim of pale yellow at the horizon faded. For the first evening since we'd arrived the sky was cloudless. Insect-eating birds swooped shrilly over the meadow. Small rustles among the dry grass told us that the night animals had awakened. A long way off we could hear the faint yawning howl of a larger animal. One by one the stars came out.

"That's Cassiopeia, isn't it?"

"No, I . . . I don't recognize it."

"If we're still in the northern hemisphere we should see Ursa Major, shouldn't we?"

"Or Orion."

"Not in summer. Not in northern latitudes."

"Maybe we're in the southern hemisphere. South America, Australia."

"Then we should see the Southern Cross. You can't miss it, if it's up there."

We tilted back our heads and stared. The stars pulsed, enormous, hanging like lanterns in the unpolluted air.

But there were not as many as I had expected. There were large patches of blackness, empty except for minute smudges of light.

"Other galaxies," said Paul, and his voice trembled.

"But where's the Milky Way? You can see at least part of it from anywhere on Earth, can't you? Well, can't you, Paul?"

Paul didn't reply. He was staring toward the east where a finger of light poked above the horizon.

"What is it? Like a searchlight."

"People. A city!"

But the finger became a column, a great column of stars clustered so tightly together that the center was a single blaze of light. Beyond the fierce glow they seemed to thin out. We could see the separate stars. It was like a pillar of light surrounded by fireflies. It was more beautiful than anything I had ever seen. Beside me Paul was shivering, although the night was very warm.

We stared in silence for a long time. Finally Brad spoke. "Paul, what *is* it?"

"I think it's the Milky Way galaxy."

"But it never looked like *this* before."

"We've never seen it from here before."

"Here? What do you mean? Paul, don't scare us."

His voice wobbled. "I'd guess that we're somewhere at the very extremity of one of the trailing arms. Looking right into the heart of our galaxy."

"What are you *talking* about? Even I remember that Earth is somewhere in the middle of the Orion arm." My voice shook.

Paul didn't answer.

Slowly the truth dawned. "You mean . . . this *isn't* Earth?"

"Of course it isn't," he burst out. "It's obvious, isn't it?" He was on his feet, turning on us. "Don't you *see*? We're on another planet. Somewhere else in the galaxy."

His voice was swallowed up in the emptiness of the incredible night. Slowly the pillar of light arched upward until it bisected the alien sky.

NINE

June 2155. Out of the Egg

I read once, in the shabby library of the city in that far-off place called Earth, that people who are suffering from terminal diseases go through distinct stages of denial, anger, self-pity, and resignation. Each of us, to a greater or lesser degree, went through the same stages.

We began by turning on Paul. "You're making this up. You've forgotten what the star charts look like."

"Liar, liar."

"You always were a show-off." This, from Trent, was grossly unfair. Whatever Paul might be, sulky, sometimes spiteful, he was never a show-off.

His face, against the blazing starlight, was white, like a tragic mask stretched over his bones. "I wish I *had* forgotten. I wish to heaven I was making it up."

"At least admit you *could* be wrong, Paul. It's only a guess, isn't it? Out of books. When did we ever have a chance to really look at the stars before? You always said we could be in South America or Australia. I bet this is the way the stars look from the southern hemisphere."

I was sitting next to Paul and I heard his sigh. It wasn't a "Lord how stupid you all are" kind of sigh. It was a sigh of pain, as if something quite final and intolerable had happened to him, like a knife through the heart.

I put my hand over his. It was like ice, although it was a midsummer night. "Paul, is there any way you can prove it?"

"Proof? You don't think *that's* proof?" He flung up his hand to the slash of dazzling white that split the dark sky like a scimitar.

"Not to me, boy." Rich's voice was thick and ugly. "Not in a blue moon."

Paul stiffened and turned to stare at Rich. "What about any kind of moon?"

"What?"

"How long have we been here?"

"Twenty-five days, isn't it? Count the notches on the tree over there."

"Almost a month. Have any of you seen the moon? By day or night? *Ever?*"

We were silent.

"It's been overcast or raining a lot of the time," said Brad at last. "And we've never been out at night before."

"All right. So just possibly the dark of the moon coincided with fine weather. From now on we'll watch. Every evening until the moon rises. If it does. But it won't. I know it won't. Then you're going to *have* to believe me, because the moon's visible from everywhere on Earth."

None of us said a word. After a long time Scylla got to her feet and swung her long hair behind her shoulders. She walked slowly back to the lean-to, stirred the fire into life, and piled wood on it until it blazed like a little sun, blotting out the cold light of the alien stars. That was *her* only denial.

"Come and get warm," she said. "I wish I could make us some cocoa, like in the old days. But come and get warm anyway."

I slept badly that night. I suspect we all did. When I woke with the sun shining in my eyes and the birds twittering in the trees I thought it had been a bad dream. Until I went outside and the great mound of ashes in our fireplace told me that it had all really happened.

I raked the ashes to one side, blew new life into the coals still glowing at the heart of the fire, and replenished it, stick by stick. Automatically I set a pot of water to heat and watched while the bubbles rose. As soon as it boiled, I threw a handful of coarse grain we had collected onto the surface and stirred.

Water still boiled, I told myself. And porridge was always porridge. I was Lisse, alive, with my friends, whether we were dreaming or in South America or . . . or somewhere else.

One by one the others wakened, came out, and stretched. I spooned hot cereal into the clay bowls we had made. Food from our fire, with our gleaned grain, eaten out of our bowls. Our living was precarious, but it was all ours, owing nothing to anyone else. I felt at the same time proud and very lonely.

"All right, Paul. Suppose you *are* right." Brad ran his hand through his hair. He had always cut his hair unfashionably short and it was odd to see it now, standing up in a shock as he ran his fingers through it. "If we *are* on another planet, how did we get here?"

Paul shrugged. "I don't know."

"We went to Barton Oaks, to the gray room with the chairs. It was no different from any other time." But Katie was denying something.

"No, you're wrong," I blurted out. "It *was* different. At least for me. I remember half waking up and there was a sense of pressure. And a feeling of being tied down. Then, when we got here . . . oh, don't you remember?"

The others stared blankly at me, and then slowly I could see them remembering too.

"Like breaking out of an egg," Paul said hesitantly.

"Like a huge bubble, white and round."

"But why had we forgotten?"

"Post-hypnotic suggestion," Rich said firmly.

"You agree it's not real, then?" Trent challenged. "We are still in Barton Oaks, aren't we?"

"Oh, Trent—"

"Don't start again." Brad got to his feet. "The only way we'll ever have peace of mind is to get this settled once and for all. Let's bank up the fire, take food and water for a couple of days, and look for that egg thing."

"What's the point? Trekking all that way for nothing. There'll be nothing there. You've been dreaming."

"We have to go. We've got to find the truth, otherwise uncertainty will fester inside us like a thorn under a fingernail. And we've all got to go. Rich and Alden. And you too, Trent."

"We don't know where it is, do we?"

"Somewhere east of the mesa. Remember, we saw the mesa in the distance," Paul reminded us.

It was a long walk to the mesa and it took us almost all that day. Katie was one of the best climbers and had the best eyes, so she shinned up to the top while we made a fire and cooked a meal. We'd sleep overnight at the mesa and look for the egg the next morning.

She was out of breath when she reached the bottom. "There *is* something. Almost due east. It wasn't there before, when we made our map."

"How far?"

She shrugged and warmed her hands at the fire. "Hard to tell in the twilight. Maybe three miles." She looked across the desert land. "It was beautiful in the last of the sun," she said softly. "Glowing like a pearl."

It still looked like a pearl the next morning. We could see it outlined against the flat desert for some time before we reached it. Nobody said anything, but we all walked more quickly until, by the time we were within a few hundred yards of it, we were running.

It was a smooth oval, its surface broken only by the circular hole through which we had emerged like unfledged birds. The door had fallen from it hinges and lay in the grass.

"Did we break it off?"

"I don't remember. Why would we have?"

"Look at this!" Alden knelt by the fallen door. As we crowded around we could see that a wiry thorn bush was actually growing up through it, reaching toward the sun as if the white plastic weren't there.

"How could that happen, Alden?"

He prodded the plastic and it gave beneath his fingers like putty. "It's a biodegradable plastic. Sensitive to ultraviolet, I suppose."

"If we hadn't remembered . . . if we hadn't come back now . . . why, in another year there'd have been nothing left. We'd never have known for sure."

Alden nodded. "Right, Lisse. Just a greener patch where the grasses were fertilized by the urea compounds. Nothing else."

I walked around our natal egg. On the far side, away from the exit, there was a tangle of plastic cord on the ground. It was soft and gummy to the touch. I traced its path along the sandy ground and found the remains of fabric, small tatters of it fluttering from the thorn bushes. I called the others.

"Drogue parachutes, attached to a cradle of cords," Brad guessed. "Nobody landed us here. We were dropped."

We stared up at the empty sky. Even Rich, Alden, and Trent were past denying the obvious now.

"Why did none of us remember the egg before?"

"Post-hypnotic suggestion again," said Rich. "They didn't want us to have the use of any Earth artifacts. That's evident, isn't it? Not a tool, nor even a box of matches. Nothing but our coveralls and boots. I suppose we should be grateful to the authorities for not dropping us stark naked." He managed a painful smile.

"But *why*? Nobody *asked* us if we wanted to leave Earth. Nobody even told us. YOU HAD NO RIGHT!"

Trent suddenly screamed at the empty sky. "NO RIGHT AT ALL!"

Trent's raised fists brought home the awful reality to us, even more than the sight of our galaxy had done. This was forever. Nobody had landed with us, helped us set up shelter, given us supplies, promised to come back in a year or so before shaking our hands and leaving. Nobody had done that. We had been thrown off Earth, dropped with nothing but our wits and our will to live. Abandoned on an alien world. Forever. And ever.

I screamed my anger to the sky. I screamed until my throat was sore. Hot tears poured down my face. Who had done this to me? Why had they done it? What had I done to deserve this fate? It wasn't fair. Simply not fair.

The others wept too. Or screamed or cursed. I'm not sure. I was deaf to anyone's suffering but my own. In the end I dropped to the ground, exhausted, with no more tears to shed. Strangely enough, it was Rich's arm around me that comforted me.

"Come on," said Scylla at last. She dragged herself to her feet. "We must go home before it gets dark."

Home! A roughly made lean-to of fallen branches. A fire painfully acquired from a flint's spark. A collection of amateurish baskets and unfired pots.

We had laid snares on the previous evening and when we reached the forest Brad reminded us that some of them might have been sprung. Numbly we walked the familiar runs and found two fat blue-furs. I found myself thinking, through a fog of self-pity, that if we were to be trapped on this planet forever, we had better start to name things. We couldn't spend the next forty years or so talking about the "big nut tree" and the "little nut tree," the "striped fish" and "blue-furs."

The next forty years. We had just got back to camp and I was raking out the fire when the words hit me. *Forty years.* A lifetime. I felt sick and my hands trembled so hard I had to stop. Benta held me close, her warm hands over my icy ones. Later that evening it was she who broke down and it was my turn to sit with my arm about her shoulder, sharing her awful loneliness.

We drifted like half-dead creatures through the next few days. We existed as marginally as we had done when we first landed, hand to mouth, grubbing for roots and berries. No one bothered to put out any more snares and no one had the heart to go fishing. The only thing we never failed to do was to keep the fire going, and we huddled close to it, staring out across the water meadow to the alien forests beyond.

Why had we not allowed ourselves to see just how alien they were? The shape of the leaves was not familiar, the grasses were not like Earth grasses, the small mammals not like any we knew. Over and over Katie and Benta had said: I don't recognize this. . . .

But we had never guessed. I suppose it was partly because our experience had been so limited. There had been Government school for ten long years. And then the city for a year, from one spring to the next. A city that was, anyway, treeless and grassless, from which we could not even see the stars at night for the golden fog of streetlights.

We shied away from the night, from the beauty of the galaxy slashed brilliantly across the dark sky. None of us took up Paul's challenge to watch for the sight of a familiar moon. We knew now that we would never see that shadowy face with the lopsided grin looking down at us. Friendly moon. Familiar moon. Not ever again.

It was lucky for us that the weather continued warm and dry or we might have died of apathy, we had so little will to live. Yet it was the smallest and silliest of incidents that brought us out of our depression.

Rich was sitting, one morning, with his back against his favorite tree, his eyes shut. Unknown to him a bird, obviously intent on nest-building, landed by his foot and tried to make off with his boot lace. Obviously it didn't succeed, but before it flew off in disgust it did succeed in undoing it. I couldn't help smiling and saw smiles on the faces of the others too.

"Wait for it." Karen chuckled.

Rich woke up, got to his feet, tripped over his trailing lace, and went sprawling.

Anything would have done, I suppose. At any rate we laughed until we hurt, until we were holding our aching sides and different tears, healing tears, were running down our cheeks.

We looked at each other, really looked this time, and saw our unkempt hair, our faces dirty and drawn, our stained clothes.

"This is terrible," Scylla exclaimed. "What have we been thinking of? Come on. Lisse and I are going fishing. The rest of you, see how many berries you can get and set some snares. As soon as we have enough food for a feast we are all going to bathe and wash our clothes."

"Where? How?"

"In the river, of course. We can beat our clothes on stones till they're clean. Yes, and scrub ourselves with sand to get this grime off. It's disgusting. The sun's hot today. Our coveralls will soon dry. I think one of the first things we must do after that is make soap. Is it hard to make soap, Alden?"

"N-no. I don't think so. Lye and fat. Lye you get from wood ash."

We looked down at the mound of ash that we hadn't bothered to rake aside and burst out laughing again. "Well, we've got plenty of that."

Scylla and I caught enough fish for twenty people and the others brought back baskets of berries. Then the boys went downstream and we went upstream and scrubbed ourselves and every stitch of clothing we had, and washed our hair.

"Goodness, the water's cold, considering the sun's on it. I wonder where it comes from."

"We'll look for the source one day," Scylla promised.

"Yes, one day we will." I smiled back. One day out of a lifetime of days. The thought was no longer terrifying but comforting. This was a world of infinite possibilities and we had hardly scratched the surface.

"I can't believe how stupid we've been," Scylla exclaimed, when we were feasting later. "Giving in the way we did."

"Long ago, after the second major war of the twentieth century," Karen said, "when they opened the concentration camps, some of the prisoners had to be coaxed out of the gates. They had been there so long, become so inured to its horrors, that the world outside no longer had any meaning for them."

"Beyond the prison gate." I lay back on the soft grass, clean and tingling, and let the sun soak into my body. "Earth *was* a kind of prison, wasn't it? And now we can do whatever we choose."

"However wild." Katie laughed.

"Except that . . ." I stopped, not knowing how to say what I was thinking.

"Go on, Lisse."

"Whatever we choose to do will become the norm for this planet, if we *are* the only people here. So we should be careful and choose wisely. So we don't wind up like Earth."

The sun set and, without making an issue of it, we stayed up, banking the fire so that we could see the night sky.

"I still don't understand why the Government—back on Earth—went through all that nonsense of The Game before bringing us here," objected Rich.

"It must have had some purpose." That was Brad.

"Maybe it was a kind of testing system, to weed out the

kind of people who wouldn't make a go of it. Think how
The Game worked; we had to learn to cooperate, to
become something stronger than each of us alone, to
become . . . well, a tribe."

"We were almost that together in our castle, weren't
we, Scylla?" I put in eagerly.

Scylla nodded. "Which is probably why we were
picked in the first place."

For a minute I had a flash of that maze with little rats
running around in it while, above, a huge human face
watched. I could feel myself getting angry and I told
myself firmly: you don't have to be angry or afraid again.
They're not watching. Not anymore.

Trent was talking. "That's all very well. But afterward,
when they knew we were suitable, why didn't they *ask*
us? It's so arrogant."

"Would you have said yes? Of course not! What about
you, Alden? Rich?" Karen challenged.

"Good grief, no."

"Not at any price."

"There you are then. And suppose you knew what was
going on, that there was a space colonization program to
get rid of excess unemployed young people, would you
have been able to keep quiet about it, if you chose not to
go?"

Trent scowled. "I don't see that—"

"It would have been a political hydrogen bomb. Can
you imagine what the workers would do if they knew
that their tax dollars were being used to send unem-

ployeds to new planets? No, I can see that it *had* to be secret, for dozens of good reasons."

"Why *us*, I wonder?"

"Perhaps we were picked even while we were in school. Perhaps that's why they *had* Government schools, so they could keep an eye on our progress. I'll bet some of you, at least, were refused jobs because they wanted you in The Game. Haven't you noticed how your skills fit this new world?" I turned eagerly from one to the other.

"You mean, I *could* have been a chemist?"

"Maybe so, Alden, but think of how much more important your skills are to us here, not just in chemistry but in inventiveness. And Brad—well, we all know that Brad can turn his hand to anything. You're the practical one, Brad."

"Yes, and Scylla's the artistic creator. It was you who thought of weaving, Scylla," Benta chimed in.

"And you've always been the one who held us together. And stopped us fighting," I went on.

"Mother Scylla," suggested Karen and we all laughed. But looking at Scylla, sitting serenely in our midst, I knew it was no joke.

"What about me?" Paul grimaced. "I'm not a lot of use on a new world."

"But you *are*. You're our memory and you're music, although you've hidden that side of yourself away in all your anger." I spoke without thinking and flushed, afraid he would indeed flare up at me, but he didn't. He just nodded quietly.

I went on, encouraged. "Katie's a geologist and biologist. Without you, Katie, we'd never have found the clay for our pots or the flint for our fire. And Karen's the historian—"

"Now that really is a dead subject in a new world."

"No, Karen, I don't think so." Scylla leaned forward. "We learn by our mistakes. There haven't *been* any mistakes here yet. It's all new. History is where we *can* learn not to make those mistakes again."

"All right, Genius. Expound on my usefulness in this brave new world." Trent challenged me and I found myself flushing again.

Here goes, I thought. "I think they're the ones who are clever—the ones who chose us to be a tribe. You're the essential grit in the system, Trent."

The others laughed and Benta said, "You have to feed grit to chickens to keep them healthy."

"There you are, Trent. You're to keep us healthy, stop us from getting smug. And Benta, you've already taught us to feed ourselves here. I'm glad they brought you from the farm. How do you feel about it now?"

Benta looked around and sighed, then smiled. "I'll miss Dad. Knowing I'll never see him again, it's as if he suddenly died. But I wouldn't miss this for anything. A new, clean world. How lucky we are!"

"Lucky!" Rich exploded. "I wish the hell they'd forgotten about *me*."

"I'm sorry, Rich. But don't you think you might have become bored after a few years of listening to the same complaints, finding the same neuroses, year after year back on Earth? You'd have burned out."

"Maybe. But I'd have been important. And the money was fantastic."

"Money for what?"

"Travel. Good food. Uncrowded accommodation—"

He stopped at our laughter. "All right, all right. I grant you I've traveled farther than I expected. *And* it's certainly uncrowded here. But as for the food—Hey, stop! I didn't mean it. It was great fish, fantastic, honestly. But I still say that I'd kill for a steak."

"If you really want one, that's what you'll have to do, Rich. No supermarkets here." Brad grinned.

After we'd settled down again, Paul got us back on track. "So why this scheme? And how did the Government do it?"

"The 'why' is simple," Karen answered. "Overcrowding. No jobs. An explosive situation getting worse. I don't think they ever realized, when they invented the robots to take over after the population fell so drastically, that it would be impossible to get rid of them once things got better. It's a problem governments have always had. You can't go back and undo things—you have to go on, it seems, even if the mess just gets worse and worse."

"I suppose we unemployeds were the real danger. The alkies, the psychedel addicts, and the real criminal elements could be kept under control by the thought police. But we were the kind of people who *had* the capacity to shake things up, to cause trouble. We were both the danger to the stability of the Government *and* the best possible candidates for seeding a new world. What's the matter?" Karen had interrupted me with a sudden movement.

"Something struck me. I've often wondered why the average life span of the population dropped from eighty-one to sixty, given all the advances in medicine and so on. Now I think I know. How do you suppose the Government keeps the books straight every time ten or twenty of us are shipped off to a new planet?"

We stared blankly at Karen.

Alden got it first. "If the program is secret, the simplest thing would be to write off the colonists as 'dead'."

"Exactly. And *that's* what's skewed the mortality figures so drastically."

"But, Karen, look! For the age of 'dying' to have dropped from eighty-one to sixty over the last few years, that's got to mean that thousands of young people are being shipped out . . . thousands."

"Yes, it does, doesn't it?"

"They wouldn't all be shipped to different planets, would they? That'd be crazy. There probably aren't that many . . ." Brad leapt to his feet. "They'd be shipped *here*, wouldn't they? It's reasonable, isn't it? Then we're not alone, after all."

"But how far away are they? This planet looks and feels very much like Earth. If we're in the equivalent of northern Michigan, the next group could be as far away as New York or Oklahoma."

"Wouldn't it have made more sense if they'd dropped us off together?"

"Not if they're hoping for diversity. The more groups struggling to survive independently, the more discoveries, the more inventions, the more chances that the colonization will succeed."

"A robot ship," Brad suggested, "with lots of little eggs, each with ten settlers. Flying low, dropping them evenly over the countryside."

"Like a farmer sowing seed," put in Benta. "Perhaps not so far apart, after all. I think we *are* intended to meet other groups. Marry into them, so that our population won't become ingrown."

I smiled inwardly. Practical Benta! And I knew she was right, remembering my feelings toward Brad and how they had changed once the group came together.

"What an undertaking!" Rich whistled. "But I still don't understand all the elaboration of The Game. Why all that nonsense about a treasure hunt? With clues and a prize."

"Some prize!"

"Don't knock it, Trent. Hundreds of acres of untouched land that's all ours."

"Clues!" My voice squeaked with excitement. "Of course the clues are important! They must have had robot explorers before they chose this planet—low-level robots with cameras. That's what they played back to us in The Game. Even though those were only sensory-enhanced dreams, they were still about *real* places. We know that already. Everything we observed when we were playing The Game is actually a part of this planet!"

"Clues to surviving here—you're right, Lisse, of course you are!"

We began to list them. There was salt to season our stews and to cure meat and fish, and goodness knows what other chemicals that Alden might find in Salt Lake. There was native copper and iron from the meteor crater—we could have real stewing pots at last. Honey. Grain from the grasslands and clay, which we had already begun to make use of. We had the essential ingredients to begin a real life for ourselves. To start building a new civilization.

Denial, anger, self-pity, and resignation. We had passed through all these stages and we mourned the death of our lives on Earth. But there was a final stage that I had forgotten. Acceptance.

That's where we were now. We hadn't cheated. We had played The Game and the prize was in our hands. What a prize! A whole world, new and unspoiled, like a landscape directly after a snowfall, before the footprints and wheel ruts, the thaw and the mud. The more I thought about it, the more I wanted to make sure that we didn't mess up *this* planet the way humans had ruined Earth. Only what could I possibly do about it? We had talked about our capabilities and the reasons why we had been chosen. But why me? What possible skill had I to offer the group?

TEN

June 2157. Prize

It is summertime again and two years have passed since we learned the truth about Prize. Prize is the name we gave this planet. It was a kind of joke at first, but it has come to mean much more than that. Each day we move a little forward. Each day is even more worth living.

I have been working on a project of my own, down where the river flows clean and fast over a gravel bed, just before it slows to meander through the water meadow. I have been soaking grasses, the stems of coarse herbs and leaves from a plant a little like an iris, until they are soft. Now, chopped, they are in a big pot of water and I am beating and rinsing them until nothing is left but the soft fibers. It is an arduous job, and I can only spare a couple of hours a day from my other activities, but I enjoy it. It requires no thought at all, so while my muscles are busy my mind wanders where it will.

This pot is beautiful, strong, well-fired, decorated with cross-hatched diamonds and rings that show up black against the reddish clay. It is one of the pots that we made over a year ago, when we still used an open fire, drying the pots thoroughly, placing them on a cradle of branches and then building up a fire over them. I am always amazed that, no matter what we make and how laborious the process is, what we make is beautiful. We are all finding within ourselves sources of expression that must have been driven far inside us back on Earth.

We have a real kiln now, made of a wattle shell daubed over with clay, and we are baking bricks. When we have enough of them we will make a furnace; then at last we will be able to extract iron from the fragments scattered around Meteor Crater. At the moment we are using beaten copper for pots and utensils, but soon we will be able to cast tools and pots and have much stronger implements, such as plows.

Not long ago Katie identified a source of tin less than twenty miles away. That means we will be able to make bronze and produce things that will last forever. We have been reliving the discoveries and inventions of our remote ancestors, only speeded up enormously so that we will move from the Stone Age to the Bronze in less than five years.

There is a great deal of iron lying around and inside Meteor Crater, but without a high-temperature furnace there is little we could do with it; its greatest use has been as a fire starter. With iron and flint we can make a fire so easily that we no longer worry about guarding it as we did in the early days. Each of us carries a small leather bag containing iron, flint, and a starter of soft dry wood or moss, just as people on Earth carry matches or a lighter.

I wonder how far we *will* go. Iron Age. And what then?

Our memories hold all the discoveries of humankind: coal, gas, oil, electricity, fission power. Pollution. The end of the line. Pollution caused the sudden drop in fertility that nearly destroyed human life on Earth. It was only the robots that saved us, becoming our hands and feet and brains when there weren't enough humans left. Then we recovered and couldn't get rid of them. The Government was faced with a choice: get rid of the robots or get rid of the young people. It's ironic that it was easier to get rid of the young people. It all has to do with the use of power. We hope we won't make the same mistakes. We are careful and we talk a lot about what went wrong with Earth.

I pound at my potful of mush, up and down, up and down. Now it has become a creamy mass, smelling of dry grass and sunshine. It's almost ready. I mix in a little white clay and pound on, straighten my shoulders, look up at the sky, and breathe deeply.

What a dazzling blue! Here on Prize the only pollution to be seen is the single thread of smoke rising unwaveringly from the kitchen fire. Yesterday we shot one of the deer-like creatures we call quadhorns. Arrows, tipped with copper or razor-sharp flints and flighted with desert-eagle feathers, are far more accurate and easier to use than spears.

When I came down to the river this afternoon, the skin had already been scraped clean of flesh and fat and Benta and Trent were rubbing it with a mixture of ash and the animal's brains. This has been a good year; already we have almost enough skins for winter clothing for us all and extra bedding for cold nights.

The quadhorn's favorite grazing is a bush like rosemary that grows near the edge of the great lake about ten miles away. Its flesh becomes permeated with the flavor of the herb and, at this time of year, is very tender. Later in the year we will hunt the older beasts and dry or salt their flesh for winter. We waste nothing.

My mouth waters at the thought of food. I pick up the pot and balance it on my head, steadying it with one hand as I walk carefully up the steep bank to the top of the bluff. From there I can see our settlement a little over half a mile away.

There is the Big House, which is our kitchen, workshop, and meeting place all in one. Behind it cluster the ten small houses, each one made of logs laid horizontally, the upper surface of each grooved so that it acts as a bed for the log above. Even without caulking no wind comes inside our log houses. Each has a door with beaten copper hinges and latch, and shuttered windows facing north to the river. The lintel posts are carved with each family's designs. For we are families now, not just tribe.

Some day soon we will start experimenting with glass. There is good fine sand out there in the desert, soda at Salt Lake, and plenty of ash left over from our fireplace, even when we have taken off the finest to make lye for our soap. For the time being, when the rain is heavy or the wind blows out of the north, we close the shutters tight and light our rooms with pottery lamps, a wick of finely plaited tree bark floating in flaxseed oil. It is not really flax, of course, but a plant like it that yields both fiber for clothing and seeds rich in oil for cooking and lighting.

I walk slowly toward the village, walking tall against the weight of the pot on my head. Now I am close enough to see the quadhorn turning on the spit above the fire. Trent and Benta have finished curing the hide and have propped it, on its stretcher, against the side of the Big House.

The others have been spreading tie-dyed cloth over the bushes to dry, so that the landscape is suddenly transformed by banners of blue and white. Once it has dried it will be cut and sewn into the loose pajama-like clothing we wear all summer and which serves as underclothing in winter, beneath leggings and jackets of quadhorn hide.

The blue dye comes from a root that grows plentifully along the sandy bluffs. Chopped and boiled in water and mixed with some of the greenish salt recovered from White Lake, it makes a powerful dye that will color our cloth in shades that vary, as the pigment becomes exhausted, from navy to the color of the sky on a fall day.

Weaving is an occupation for evenings and for the winter months when we don't spend as much time out of doors. Brad and Scylla designed a four-harness loom that yields a fine narrow cloth from which we can make our clothing with a minimum of cutting and sewing. Since the others came, we have built a second loom.

We all spin thread whenever we have a little time to spare between chores, and all winter the best weavers work, turning out lengths of cloth that are stored until midsummer, when the blue-roots are ready. By the end of next week we will all have new clothes to wear for the celebration of the first anniversary of Meeting, which coincides with Midsummer Day.

It is strange and terrifying to think that if it had not been Midsummer we might not have met them, although eventually I suppose our paths must have crossed. We talked often enough of looking for another group, but there was always so much work to be done, and where were we to start?

It began one evening, as we sat watching the Milky Way rise above the eastern horizon.

"It's been a year since our coming. We should celebrate," Scylla had said.

"Let's have a feast!" exclaimed Rich. The discovery of the quadhorn had been the turning point of his life on Prize.

"Let's go back to the very beginning—to the mesa."

"What a great idea, Lisse! Let's dress up in our best clothes and take firewood and a feast with us."

"We could do it every year, beginning now. To give thanks. Forever and ever."

So it was that at dawn on the longest day of the year we set out, all ten of us, laden with meat, roots, fruit, honeycake, and berry wine, on the day-long trek across the desert to the mesa. We planned to feast that evening, watch the stars rise, and sleep out, as we had had to do in those first days.

We arrived in the late afternoon and began to prepare the fire on the shady eastern side of the mesa. Brad and Paul decided to climb to the top while the rest of us prepared the feast. I remember I was chopping yellow-roots when Paul yelled and my flint knife slipped and sliced into the ball of my left thumb. I wrapped a cloth around it and ran back with the others to where we could crane our necks up to the summit of the mesa.

"What's the matter?" we yelled.

"*People*!" He and Brad were pointing over to the east. We turned, but could see nothing.

"Over by the forest," Brad yelled.

"What'll we do? We can't just let them go."

"Bonfire. On top of the mesa."

We'd been a team for so long that it took few words to get us organized. Brad let down a rope. Firewood was bundled together and hauled to the top of the mesa while Paul got a small fire started.

"It's too dry. Send up some damp grass."

"It's all bone dry."

"Send it up anyway."

The rest of us stared alternately at the eastern horizon and anxiously up at the top of the mesa. Suddenly a pillar of smoke rose straight and true into the clear sky.

"You've done it! They can't possibly miss *that*!"

Puffs of smoke rose one by one into the sky. Even from the edge of the forest to the east the strangers must have seen and understood that they were looking at no accidental fire. Brad and Paul climbed down the mesa and landed beside us.

"How *did* you manage to get that grass wet? It was as dry as tinder."

Brad and Paul grinned at each other.

"Come on. There wasn't a drop of water up there—Oh!" I blushed.

"That's right. We peed on it. Highly effective."

The laughter broke the tension and we busied ourselves with preparations for the feast. There had probably never been so many cooks at a time around a single fire.

By the time the quadhorn's skin was brown and splitting, so that the fat ran glistening down the sides to flare on the hot embers beneath, we could all see the strangers, ten dark dots that slowly elongated, became people. Then we could see the color of their clothes, not like ours, made of papery stuff, brown and ornamented with white and red paint. I felt suddenly shy, they were so different, almost foreign.

We were all on our feet now, staring at them. Then we moved forward toward them and stopped. They stopped too, and we stared at each other. The only sound on the whole of Prize seemed to be the crackle and hiss of the fat dripping into the fire behind us. Then, above our heads, a desert eagle swooped and screamed and the spell was broken. We ran toward each other, our arms outstretched. We met and hugged one another.

How strange it was to feel an unfamiliar body, to smell a foreign smell, the faintly bitter scent of bark-cloth. To look up into a pair of laughing gray eyes that I had never seen before. I remember drawing back, blushing, trembling, and being pulled into yet another embrace.

Now, nearly a year later, it is hard to remember that there was a time when I didn't know Philip, my husband.

We gathered around the fire in the twilight. We ate luscious slices of quadhorn until our faces shone with grease. The newcomers shared with us the waybread they were carrying with them, flat bread, and early groundberries. And we talked. We never stopped, except to swallow and bite off another piece of meat or bread.

We found that in the original Game the new ten had not started out, as we had, at the mesa, but at an oasis, fed by an artesian spring, some thirty miles to the east. This Midsummer Day, when we had trekked out to the mesa, they had been hunting at the extreme southwest of their territory. It was only by the slightest chance that we had met at all.

We had both come to Prize in the same "seeding." It seemed likely, we decided, that our robot carrier had come to Prize only once, scattering our eggs, not evenly across the planet as we had guessed at first, but in clusters, so that we might meet after a time, when our original bonded groups had become strong, and after we had made some discoveries and inventions but not become so set in our ways that the others would have felt like intruders.

They were very clever, the people who had designed The Game. They even understood that the ten who arrived together on an alien planet *would* become a bonded group, as close to each other as brothers and sisters. We had become kin. Any other relationship would have been distasteful.

But now there was a new group and all was well. And all has been well. In the last year each of us has married one of the other ten. We spend most of the year here on the sandy bluffs above the water meadow, but in future we plan to winter at the oasis, where it is warmer and where there is plenty of fresh fruit throughout the cold weather. The tin we discovered is not far from the oasis, and we plan to build our furnace close to it, far enough away from the oasis that there will be no pollution.

I have reached the village now and swing my pot down from my head to the ground outside our house, Philip's and mine. I touch the lintel as I enter; Philip and I carved the designs together, of leafy creepers interlacing butterflies and the birds we call peewits. I wipe the sweat from my forehead with my sleeve. It is cool in here, smelling of the rush mats on the floor. The bed is a wooden frame, laced with leather cords, the mattress stuffed with cotton. Above is a quilt, fat with podfluff. There is a chest for our belongings and two stools. It is both simple and beautiful. We have discovered something wonderful on Prize: that there need be no separation between what used to be called "work" and "play." We do everything as well and as joyfully as we can and it turns out to be beautiful.

Propped in a corner is the basketwork cradle I was twining before I began this project. There is plenty of time to finish it. Beside it is a frame with a mat of finely split reeds sewn together and fastened rigidly to it. Upon this sits a second empty frame. Unknown parsecs away, in the shabby city library back on Earth, there was a section called "Arts and Crafts" where I used to browse. I think I remember how to do it. I hope I remember.

I go outside and, holding the double frame firmly together with both hands, I dip it into the mush in the pot. I bring it up, dripping, shake it back and forth, side to side. I put it on the ground to drain for a while, so that the water runs between the reeds, leaving behind the fiber residue.

Now I take off the loose upper frame and turn the reed sieve upside down over a pad of undyed cloth. When I lift it, holding my breath, an oblong of creamy mush remains behind. I lay another cloth over it, dip the double frame into the mush once more, and repeat my actions, until I have a pile of alternate layers of mush and cloth. When I have finished, I put a flat board over the pile and put some big rocks on top and leave them to dry.

Later I go back to the pile and lift off the sheets of paper I have made and lay them carefully in the sun. This is the first thing I have made that is entirely mine from beginning to end. I feel sure of myself, as if I were a different person from the frightened Lisse who took a bus from school to the city. Now, when I look back at that girl, it seems to me that we have nothing at all in common.

When the tie-dyed cloth is dry, we cut it up and begin to sew our new garments. Very early on Midsummer morning we start out for the mesa, laden with food and firewood. We light a bonfire on top of the mesa and cover it with damp straw that we have brought, wrapped in mats, from the grassland. White smoke rises thickly in the air. We take turns tending this signal fire throughout the afternoon. If any other group is within sight, they may join us. We plan to set the fire every year on this day.

We feast. We talk over the year that has gone by. I tell it in story and Paul rhymes it into song. Jon, from the second group, makes musical instruments, pipes and stringed instruments to pluck. We all play and sing. The night passes quickly as we watch the galaxy rise in the east and arch overhead in all its familiar splendor. How lucky we are, I think, as I lean against Philip's shoulder and look around at the familiar faces in the firelight: Scylla and Kev, Brad and Toni, Rich and Lillyanne, Paul and Myn, Katie and Derek, Alden and Penelope, Trent and Marcy, Karen and Todd, my dear Benta and Jon, who is Philip's brother.

When we return home the next day I gather up my dried paper and hold a sheet of it to the light. It is smooth, creamy white, crisp. I believe it will do.

It takes me the better part of the following morning to trim a feather properly, even with the small copper knife Philip has made for me. I must cut the quill at an angle, hollow its tip, and then cut in it a small vertical slit. This is where I get into trouble. I have ruined so many feathers, they litter the ground around my feet as if I have been molting. But I am determined to do this myself.

At last I achieve one that pleases me. From the wooden chest, carved with our intertwined initials and a design of water reeds in flower, I take a small clay pot with a stopper.

I squat on my heels at the door of my house and look

about me before I begin. I can smell bread baking in the clay oven. I can see the haze of smoke caught by the slanting morning sun. I can hear the ting-tang of Philip's mallet hitting and bouncing, hitting and bouncing, as he slowly beats a piece of native copper into a bowl. How happy I am.

I feel a stirring within me and my hand automatically flies to my stomach, the fingers spread. *There*. In a hundred days or so our first child will be born, Philip's and mine. The first child on Prize. The first of many.

Before that day comes I want to have a story for her. It is as important to me as finishing the cradle. I want her to know what it was like for me on Earth, long ago. I don't want to write a history with dates and names of important people, as Karen could. I don't want to write the story of Earth politics, as Trent might, although that comes into it. I don't even want to write the kind of song history that Paul makes.

This is going to be *my* story. Lisse's story, for the first girl to be born in our new home on Prize. How do I know she's going to be a girl? Philip says that's just my fancy, but I know I am right.

I dip my quill into the ink pot and hold the first sheet of paper steady with my left hand. I hold my breath as I make the first downward stroke. Will the ink run? Or will the tip of the quill catch in a rough spot on the paper and spatter?

As I draw the quill downward, the ink, compounded of dye and tree-gum, flows into a perfect "I." I settle comfortably on my knees, leaning over the paper, and slowly the smell of boiling roots and baking bread, the sound of the hammer and of voices and laughter fade away and I am back at my beginnings, writing my history for my daughter.

"It was the last day of school and . . ."

〰〰 ABOUT THE AUTHOR 〰〰

Monica Hughes is one of the most popular writers for young people, and has won numerous prizes at home and abroad. Her books have been published in Poland, Spain, Japan, France, Scandinavia, England, and Germany. She has twice received the Canada Council Prize for Children's Literature, and was runner-up for the Guardian Award.

She is the author of *Keeper of the Isis Light*, an American Library Association Best Book for Young Adults, which also received a Certificate of Honor from the International Board on Books for Young People; *Hunter in the Dark*, also an ALA Best Book for Young Adults; and *Sandwriter*, among many other titles.

Monica Hughes was born in England and now lives in Canada.